A SHIFT
IN
FIRE

PATRICIA D. EDDY

If you love sexy romantic suspense, I'd love to send you a short story set in Dublin, Ireland. Castles & Kings isn't available anywhere except for readers who sign up for my mailing list! Sign up for my newsletter on my website and tell me where to send your free book!
http://patriciadeddy.com.

PROLOGUE

The walls around her shook, and the magic that trapped her in her own body, that stopped her from moving, blinking, even breathing fell away.

She drew her shoulders inward, the pain of movement after so long bringing tears to eyes that could no longer see. Fear chilled her skin, and she rocked back and forth as best she could within the confines of the chains and the tiny stone prison that had been her home for as long as she could remember.

What was happening? The Thirteen hadn't brought the power of Earth—or any other element—to her in a very long time. So long she thought it might even have been years.

And now...she could sense it. Taste it.

There was air too. Fire. Water. They called to the fragments of the elements she carried deep inside her broken body from all the times her tormentors had tried—and failed—to turn her into their weapon.

Oh, no. Please no.

If they had all four...they would again channel them into her, bind them to her until the elements themselves broke free, tearing her apart and sending her to the brink of death. Or... close enough that she'd pray for its cold, quiet embrace to take her.

Only to have Celia—the coven leader—yank her away from the abyss shattered and broken, then blame her for a failure she knew was not hers to bear.

A low, hoarse whine—the only sound she was capable of making—filled her stone prison, and though it was pitch dark— had been for almost her entire existence as their precious conduit—she squeezed her eyes shut anyway.

Just let me die. Take me. End this existence so my soul can be free.

A chunk of rock slammed into her shoulder. She welcomed the pain, praying the next one would hit her head. Her neck. Damage her in a way that could not be repaired.

The chains rattled, her wrists bound to one another over her head. Her ankles, too, were secured, the thick cuffs attached to a ring in the floor she sometimes felt with her bare toes on the rare occasions she was allowed to move at all.

The earthquake worsened, and she tipped her head up, waiting for the next stone to fall.

But the only thing that fell? Her hands. The chain had worked its way free from the stone behind her, hitting her across the nose with a sickening crack. Blood streamed over her upper lip, and she whimpered again, her shoulders protesting the sudden, violent movement of arms that had so infrequently been allowed the freedom to do so.

Bright light seared her eyes, even through her shuttered lids, and warmth hit her cheeks. Was that...sun?

The prospect of freedom had been so far from her grasp ever since the Thirteen had taken her, she'd forgotten how much she'd loved the sun. Forgotten it even existed.

The stone floor under her naked body buckled, and one foot

flopped to the side. It took all Sameen had to reach her tingling hands—she didn't remember a time they hadn't been numb—forward, and after another few seconds, she found the ring. The rocks had released one end of it. If she tried...if she had the strength...she could free both ankles, and then she could *move*.

The stench of burnt flesh filled her nose, and she retched. Not that she had anything in her stomach. The Thirteen had slowed all of her bodily functions to the minimum ages ago. She rarely ate or drank, didn't remember the last time she'd slept, and there was something else...something she knew she'd once had to do. Oh. Yes. But that came after eating and drinking, so it was no wonder she'd forgotten it all.

Her other foot slid free, and though both ankles still bore the heavy iron cuffs and her wrists were still connected by a short chain, she was freer than she'd been since they'd taken her so long ago.

Sameen fell over and rolled onto her stomach. She couldn't see. Years of being unable to blink had scarred her eyes to the point even light and dark were hard to discern. But she could feel. And if she concentrated, she could wriggle forward a few inches at a time.

Jagged rocks—some as small as pebbles and others almost boulders—slowed her, cut into her stomach, her breasts, her thighs, but she didn't care. Something had gone horribly wrong above ground, and only two options presented themselves to her.

She could stay in her tiny stone cell with the walls shaking around her and wait for one of the Thirteen to retrieve her—assuming she survived. Or she could try to escape. The punishment would be excruciating if she were caught. But she'd suffered excruciating before. Time and time again, and risking another go on the rack where their magic made her feel like her body was being torn apart joint by joint? Where her skin burned and fell off in sheets, where each hair was yanked out one-by-one, each finger snapped, each tooth forcefully extract-ed...all to have that same magic then put her back together so they could start on her anew?

That was a risk she had to take.

She marked her progress by the amount of sunlight hitting her bare skin. First, it was just her cheeks. Then her neck. Then her shoulders. By the time her toes were bathed in the sun's warmth, she was so tired, she didn't think she could go on.

Another great quake tossed her body into the air, and she landed somewhere...else. On a carpet of moss and leaves, with the scent of the forest all around her. She remembered trees. Grass. The outdoors.

From a distance, she heard screaming and she curled into a ball.

Hide.

But where? She couldn't see, had almost no strength left, and she didn't even know what she was hiding from. Were those screams from the Thirteen? Or others who'd come to destroy them?

She huffed out what might have been a laugh if she'd been capable of sound. No one could destroy the Thirteen. They were the most powerful beings in this world—and probably the next world as well.

Her fingers brushed something leafy, and she felt her way up until she couldn't reach any higher. A bush or bramble of some sort, tall enough and she thought possibly thick enough to hide her.

Creeping her way around the thing, still only able to move on her belly, she stopped when the vegetation muffled the screams and shouts. If the branches were between her and the Thirteen, she might be safe enough to rest here until more of her strength returned.

Turning her head away from the sun, she covered her face with her bound hands and passed out.

MARA

Her body was still. Sitting up with her back against a wall, somewhere dark and cool. Mara, however, was trapped in that same tiny box she always found herself in when the *other* part of her took over.

"Help me!" she cried silently. She couldn't sense Cade at all. Where was he?

Wracking her brain, she tried to focus on her last memory. They'd been outside. In the backyard. Eli was about to try the casting. Something went wrong.

Cade grabbed her, but after that, everything went dark and fuzzy. The *other* presence occupying her body had taken over, and it was still in control now.

Oh God. Her baby. What about her baby? Did the fire even *know* she was pregnant? Did it care?

Her daughter kicked gently, almost as if she could sense Mara was about to give in to panic.

It'll be okay, sweetie. Somehow. Your daddy will find us, or we'll figure a way out of this ourselves if we have to.

If only she believed her own words. The longer she remained aware in this locked away place, the more she was able to see around her.

Bars. Metal bars. Dark stone walls. A dim light coming from a corridor, but no way out of the cell. There wasn't even a door. Just one entire wall of metal slats too narrow to squeeze through—even if she weren't pregnant.

Though the view was always a bit distorted when fire locked her away, Mara could see enough to know she—her body—wasn't anywhere good. The *other* her took a deep breath, and the scent of magic, bitter and sharp, flooded her nose.

"You have to let me out," she begged the consciousness in control. *"I won't survive if you don't. Not...wherever this is."*

Nothing. Not even a single muscle twitch.

"The baby needs me."

Mara's field of vision shrank almost down to nothing, as if the fire were actively *punishing* her for speaking up. But, even as she lost most of her very limited sight, she felt her body's arms wrap tenderly around her stomach.

If she had control of her tear ducts, she'd be bawling by now. Terrified, trapped, and with no idea where Cade was or how he'd ever find her, she wasn't sure how long she could stay locked away before she lost herself completely.

HOURS. Maybe even a day passed. Hell, for all she knew of time, it could have been two. No one had come. No food or water. No blanket or pillow. Yet she wasn't hungry or thirsty. The fire was still in control, and it hadn't let her move. Not even an inch. She stayed braced against the wall, arms around her baby bump, feeling her daughter kick and wriggle.

The smell of magic never let up. The practitioners must have spelled her. Otherwise, there was no way she'd still be in as good shape as she was without moving at all. The baby would be in distress.

Her muscles tensed, and Mara fought against the fire. *"Let me see what's happening!"* she begged, and suddenly, the entire cell came into view. *"Thank you. God, thank you. We have to be ready for anything."*

Something shifted inside of her, and she could feel emotions she knew weren't her own. They belonged to the *other* her. The fire elemental was detached. Almost aloof. But underneath that? A very small kernel of fear.

Footsteps. Slow. Multiple sets.

The bars parted—not by any mechanism, but by magic—and two large men stepped into the cell. They wore dark robes with hoods that hid the top half of their faces. Behind them, two women stood in long purple tunics and black pants. "Bring her. Do not harm the baby," one of the women ordered.

The fire elemental let out a howl, flailing her arms, kicking, trying to scramble into a corner of the cell, but the woman who'd spoken uttered a few words in a language Mara thought was Gaelic, and her muscles went slack. The men picked her up easily, one grabbing her under the arms and the other taking her legs at the ankles.

They were gentle. As gentle as they could be carrying a pregnant woman hanging between them.

Mara didn't bother trying to fight her way back from the place her sister's element had sent her. Wherever they were taking her, she wanted fire in control. Her other half was stronger, and this wasn't going to be good.

Down a long, dim corridor. The musty odor made her stomach turn, and her daughter kicked her—hard—right in the stomach. At least the spell hadn't affected the baby.

The men turned left and brought her into a large ritual space. A silver circle was inlaid into the stone floor, made up of dozens of symbols. Some, like the Celtic Trinity Knot, she recognized. Others, she'd never seen before.

Laying her on a massive stone altar in the center of the circle, the men secured her wrists and ankles in metal cuffs so her joints stretched painfully, and the other half of her consciousness whimpered.

The two women took up position close to Mara's waist. The one on the left—a blond with short, spiked hair, withdrew a small blade from her pocket and cut Mara's t-shirt from the neck to the hem.

"Bring the iron," the other practitioner said to the men, then with a few more unintelligible words, Mara's body was freed from whatever spell had kept her immobile.

"No, no, no," the fire elemental hissed. "Not the baby."

"Oh, we would never harm the baby, elemental. She—along with Eliziam Ruiz—will give us the world. Now we *could* wait another ten weeks until you give birth, or we can speed up the process."

Mara would have been hyperventilating if she'd been the one in control of her body. Nothing could *speed up* pregnancy.

"Is it hot enough?" the blond one asked. "If Celia has to perform the ceremony a second time, it will not be good for the baby."

"Aye, Mistress Freya," the man said. Mara tried to see what the robed lackey was holding, but as her head started to turn, Freya, the blond practitioner, forced a thick piece of leather between her teeth.

"You will need this, elemental. If you do not do your best to hold still, this will be immeasurably more painful." Freya's purple eyes held no emotion beyond disdain, and Celia started to chant.

"Oh, God. No. Not another spell. Please—"

"Now," Freya said, and the hooded man pressed a white-hot branding iron to Mara's side.

She—and the fire elemental—both screamed until the sizzle and stench of burnt flesh made Mara's stomach roil. Tears streamed down her cheeks, and she fought not to pass out.

Celia, whose jet-black hair was wound into a tight knot at the base of her neck, rested her hand on Mara's forehead. "That is the worst of it, elemental. The control mark will ensure you do not give us any trouble. Or harm yourself or the baby."

Control mark?

Mara strained to see what they'd done to her, but she couldn't raise her head. When the hooded man stepped back, however, panic seized her heart in a vise. The branding iron he held aloft...she recognized that symbol. It was the same one Fergus had tried to carve into Farren's side. The same one he'd given Colin. The same one the Thirteen had given Tharp all those years ago.

The fire elemental spit out the leather. "You will die for this."

"By the power of the *Cumhacht Dearadh*, we take control of this body," Celia murmured as she stared into Mara's eyes. "Time is ours, we do control, the child will not pay the toll. Pass a week now in a day, ensure the mother will obey."

Pain—like a lattice work of electricity—spread across Mara's skin, and she arched her back, tried to dig her heels against the altar, and screamed until she couldn't anymore.

Freya snapped her fingers and murmured a few quiet words, and Mara's thoughts muddled. Slowed. Her eyelids fluttered, and she had the vague idea she was moving. Standing.

A cool breeze hit her naked back, followed by the rustle of cloth cascading from her shoulders to her bare toes. The brand on her side tightened, the pain fading into her memories.

Walking now. Only the occasional brief glimpse of the stone corridor. Of a plain gray dress covering her body.

"Bring her food and water," Celia called to someone behind them. At least now Mara knew who was holding her arm. Not that she could resist. Her legs moved of their own accord, and though the fire elemental hadn't released her control yet, Mara sensed the other half of her consciousness was just as trapped and terrified as she was.

Back in the cell, when Celia let go of her, she was finally able to force her eyes open. Now, instead of being completely empty, there was a thin mattress on the floor, complete with blanket and pillow. The left wall had...*moved,* and where it had once been, a toilet and sink.

"You will do as we command," Celia said, her voice taking on a deeper, raspier tone. "Do not fight us. You will eat and drink what we bring you. All of it. When the lights go out, you will sleep. When they turn on, you will wake. You belong to us now, elemental, and once your child is born, your end will be merciful."

Merciful.

Mara took solace in that word. For all of two minutes. As soon as one of the black-robed men set a tray of food on a small wooden table and she was alone again, the bars materialized back in place before her eyes, and the fire elemental yanked up the dress and started clawing at the brand on her side.

But her nails were too short to do any damage to the mark because *it was no longer fresh.* The thick reddish scars looked to be at least a week old, maybe more, and as she felt her belly, she realized what Celia's words had meant.

The baby had *grown.* In the time it had taken the practitioners to brand her, make her change clothes, and march her back to her cell, it was almost as if a week had passed.

The fire elemental screamed, the sound full of horror and pain, and Mara fell to her knees on the mattress. Her eyes rolled back in her head, and then, like a switch had been flipped, *she* was in control again.

"Oh, baby...I'm so sorry. Rachel. Rachel Eleanor. That's what your name is. If I—God—if I don't get to raise you, if your daddy can't find us...never forget. You're Rachel Eleanor Bowman, and you are loved so much." She cradled her belly gently, rubbing circles over where she hoped her daughter would kick next, and it only took a few seconds before she was rewarded with a tiny thud against her palm.

The scent of the food hit her, and she *had* to eat. Some sort of stew, a roll, a pile of spinach. Easily three servings, yet she finished it all. Along with a large jug of water and a pint of milk. Every bite left her hungrier than the last. Until it was all gone.

The light was still on in the corridor, but she had no idea how long she'd be allowed to stay awake, how long they'd force her to sleep, or who would be in control when she woke up. So she sat on the mattress and pulled the blanket around her shoulders.

"Listen, Katerina. Or...whoever the hell you are. Katerina's spirit? Her soul? Some dormant part of me that just needed a mega-dose of fire to wake the hell up? We need to stop fighting one another and work together here. I don't even know if that's possible, but they're going to take this baby from me—from us—if we don't."

Anger stirred deep inside her. Anger she knew wasn't hers. Or, not exactly hers.

"That's right. They'll take Rachel and turn her into some sort of weapon or vessel for them to be able to harness spirit. You have been paying attention, right?"

She felt her other half's answer rather than heard it, and hallelujah. They had some basic level of communication started.

"So help me stop them. You've been taking over for months now. And no one's been able to figure out why or what you want. Find a way to tell me. Even if you have to put me back in that tiny little box again to do it. I don't care."

Something inside her started to burn, an ember deep in her chest, aching to be free, but before it could catch fire, the light went out, and though she fought with everything she had, the practitioners' spell was too strong, and she toppled over, asleep.

CHAPTER ONE

PETER

*H*is footsteps echoed on the Travertine floors, and Peter wondered why, since Regulus hadn't set foot in Scotland in more than twelve years, he felt the need to keep such a lavish home here.

Gift horse. Mouth. Who the fuck cares?

He shouldn't. Not when this house was currently protecting his family. Well, some of his family. They were spread across the globe now. Shawn, Livie, and their baby daughter in Canada. Ollie and Christine in Seattle, and Mara...

Shit. Guilt soured his stomach, and he stopped halfway through adding the coffee beans to the most expensive espresso machine he'd ever seen outside of the coffee shops in Seattle.

Cade's mate had been taken from Farren's house in Ireland less than thirty-six hours earlier. With Eli's help—Peter still had no idea how the man's unique combination of magic and elemental powers worked—they'd put an end to five practitioners and destroyed one of their lairs just a few hours ago. But the remaining members of the Thirteen—a coven dedicated to bringing about the fifth element of spirit so they could hold life and death in their hands—had hidden Mara somewhere else. Somewhere Cade couldn't sense her and no one could scry for her.

The floor shook underneath Peter's feet. Directly below, in the east wing basement, Cade, Peter's alpha, had lost his mind with worry over his mate and their unborn child. When Liam, the pack's beta, had last checked on him, he'd still been in wolf form, throwing his massive body against the stone walls time and time again.

"Ya' plannin' on blockin' that machine all day? Or can ya' move aside so I can get a cuppa?" Liam's voice startled him, and Peter dropped the bag of beans on the counter, barely stopping them from spilling all over the fucking place.

"Don't sneak up on me like that," Peter snapped. "Not today."

Liam held up his hands and took a step back. "Wasn't tryin' to, mate. Ye're off in another world."

"Not another world." Peter moved out of the way so Liam could brew two cups of coffee. "Just stuck in this shitty one and trying to figure out how the fuck we went from Bellingham eighteen months ago to here. We were happy. Safe. And now...?"

"I know." Liam ran a hand through his shoulder-length reddish hair. "I can't reconcile bein' so happy I got my Caitlin back and so shattered over losin' Mara. Or Cade bein' tortured for so many months. Or yer..."

Peter flinched. "My damage? You can say it, Liam. I'm fucked up. Can't run like the rest of you, can't even manage stairs on my bad days. I'm glad you found your mate. Hell, I'm fucking sorry for giving her such a hard time when she came back. And there's nothing I wouldn't do to find Mara. But can you blame me for wishing we could all go back in time?"

Abandoning his quest for caffeine, Peter turned, a little unsteady on his left leg, intending to stalk away, but his knee buckled, and he grabbed one of the dining room chairs so he wouldn't fall.

"When was the last time ya' slept?" Liam asked.

"Same time you did, asshole. When was the last time you checked on Cade?" Peter gritted his teeth and gingerly put weight on his bad leg.

Hold. Come on. Just hold.

Most of the time, he did okay. His wolf could manage something close to a run, though he couldn't keep up with Cade and Liam when they were at full speed. But after the fight at the Thirteen's castle just twelve hours ago, he was hurting.

Liam passed him on the way to the ornate spiral staircase in the center of the mansion. "About an hour ago. I'm goin' to take a few minutes with Caitlin and then go back down there. Maybe he'll have worn himself out by then. Get some rest."

"I can't. We're only what? Five miles from that fucking dungeon? Or...at least where it used to be before Eli destroyed it. I'm going to shift. See if I can find any hint of Mara's scent. There was too much magic surrounding the place this morning. It should have faded by now."

"Peter, ya' don't have to prove anythin' to me, ya' know. Or to Cade." Liam's green eyes held too much sadness and pain. Of all the wolves, Liam carried the most guilt for Peter's injuries. He'd been the one to get them all to safety after the fire, and even though it had been Katerina's charm that had stopped Peter from shifting and ensured his injuries would never fully heal, Liam had taken on much of the blame.

"Maybe I have to prove something to myself." Pulling his sweatshirt over his head, Peter limped towards the back door.

THE MANSION SAT in the center of what had to be a ten-acre estate. Tall spires rose to the sky, heavy leaded glass windows looked to be at least two hundred years old, and the place had two separate wings.

"Consider this your home for as long as you require," Regulus said when they arrived, beaten all to hell after their battle with five of the Thirteen's practitioners. "I ask only that you stay out of the west wing basement. The young wolf's transition will take many hours, and during that time, he is at his most lethal. Oh, and please do not tamper with the draperies. They are all motorized, so if I need to be above ground during the daylight hours, I will not...combust."

"You might not need to worry about that any longer." Eli, with his arm around Farren's shoulders, nodded at Regulus's hand. Farren's new mate could command all four elements, and—thanks to the sigils and ancient symbols he'd absorbed from a magical book—could go toe-to-toe with the strongest of the Thirteen.

Regulus stared at his burned fingers. Gold wound its way around two of them, the remnants of a signet ring one of his progeny had given him over a century ago so he could walk in the sun. Its power had faded over the years, but Eli had renewed the magic. If only the Thirteen hadn't set the vampire to flame. The gold was now permanently fused with skin and bone—or so it appeared to Peter.

"Better to be cautious," Regulus said as he carried Ewan—one of Farren's wolves—in from the garage. The boy had been killed by one of the practitioners, his neck snapped, but Regulus had turned him rather than let their group suffer yet another loss. "When the boy has fully transitioned and fed, I will bring you to see him, Farren. He should not make his final choice without speaking to you."

Farren held on to Eli like he was the only thing keeping her upright. Given that she'd turned Eli's father into a werewolf to free him from the Thirteen's endless control...Peter wouldn't blame her if she lost her shit. Plus, Ewan's...death...had been yet another blow to her pack, which now consisted of only her and Tierney.

"Thank ya', Regulus. I never thought I'd be in a vampire's debt, but I am."

"On the contrary, she-wolf. You owe me nothing, and I—" he held up his hand, "—owe you everything."

As PETER TOED off his boots and shed his jeans and briefs, he stared straight ahead, not daring to let his gaze drift to his chest —or any other part of him. The scars covered most of the left half of his body from his cheek to his calf. The last time he'd been set up on a blind date, the woman had bolted after the first drink. Gone to the bathroom and slipped out the back.

He might as well be Quasimodo. When the pack had moved to Seattle, he and Liam had started their own construction company, but Peter couldn't actually *build* anything. He'd been relegated to the office. He *hated* the office. And though he'd helped fight Fergus when the earth elemental had come after Caitlin, kidnapped Liam, and almost killed them all, though he'd fought with the rest of them just the previous day and helped take down at least one of the practitioners, he still felt like a failure.

Dropping to all fours, Peter reached for his wolf. The animal was a part of him, even though he hadn't been born a wolf. No, he'd been bitten at sixteen while camping with his Eagle Scout Troop.

His first shift—only ten minutes after he'd been bitten—had scared the crap out of him, and he'd been too afraid to go home again. He'd lived on the streets of Vancouver, Canada for two years until one full moon when he was twenty-three. He'd run so far and so fast, he'd ended up in the woods outside of Bellingham. That's where he'd met Cade, Liam, and Ollie. After that night, he'd never slept on the street again.

The moon had just risen above the horizon, and its power surged through Peter's limbs. The shift started with his back, every vertebrae cracking and healing in only a few seconds. Fur sprouted along his spine, spreading out over his ribs, and his ears sharpened into points. As his human teeth were absorbed back into his jaw and the sharp canines pierced his gums, Peter howled into the night.

The pain was excruciating, but the thrill of it…of being able to run faster and farther than his human form could ever hope, of being able to see and smell and hear *everything*…it was worth it. Every. Single. Time.

Taking off in the direction of the practitioners' former lair, Peter ignored the zings of pain that ran up and down his left hind leg. It took him twice as long as it would have taken Cade, Liam, Farren, or Tierney, but in fifteen minutes, he reached the spot where the stone building had once been.

Eli had made the whole structure disappear. Shrink in on itself and then simply…vanish. Peter had no idea how, nor did he think he ever would. Eli's powers were a mystery to Eli, let alone the rest of them.

Taking his time, Peter sniffed around the entire property. Hints of magic remained, along with Cade, Liam, and Tierney's blood. A few drops here, a few more there. And something else. Something…sweet. Intoxicating. What the hell was it?

Peter retraced his steps, and a concentrated pool of the new scent lingered not far from where he, Cade, Liam, and Caitlin had entered the dungeon. Had there been another set of cells? His lupine eyes could sense more than most humans, and he limped a hundred feet away and climbed up on a large rock angling out of the mossy landscape.

The footprint for the structure was clearly visible. As were two sets of stairs leading down to two separate collapsed dungeons.

Oh, fuck. What if Mara had been in that other underground bunker? Peter leapt off the stone, ignoring the pain in his body, and made a beeline for the second set of steps.

The sweet scent was stronger here. Peter kept his nose to the ground, nudging the dirt in several different spots. Definitely blood. Definitely not Mara's.

He took his time. Digging through the rubble until he was positive Mara had never been here. No one expected him back at the vampire's manor—at least not for hours—and on occasion over the past few months, he'd wondered if the rest of his pack gave a shit whether he was even there.

The delicious scent clung to the ground, as if it had been painted on. More than once he fought off the suspicion he was being led into a trap.

If he were, the stench of magic would be stronger. That thought kept him going as he padded slowly, carefully, following a path he was almost powerless to walk away from.

Until he came to a heavily wooded area. The trees here provided a canopy that hid much of the moon's bright, comforting light, and thick brambles scratched his legs and paws.

He would have stopped, but the scent? It was in the air now. Sweet but perfumed with fear.

And then he heard it. A sharp inhale. A quiet rustle. Movements. His wolf growled, and he tried to keep the sound inquisitive and non-threatening, but his sensitive hearing picked up a heartbeat. A racing heartbeat.

Dropping onto his belly, he prepared to shift back into his human form, but hesitated long enough to take one last, deep pull of the air so he had the scent memorized.

A slightly burnt undertone, yet hints of fresh rain, the ocean breezes, and the moss that covered everything in this area. If he didn't know better, he'd think he was scenting an elemental, but the smells were wrong. Off somehow.

Trap, remember?

He tried to convince his wolf he shouldn't shift, but the animal was desperate to know what was in the bushes only thirty feet away, and the man would be much better equipped to understand—or to communicate—if it were actually a person.

He howled as the shift overtook him. The transition back to a man was always so much harder. Mostly because at the end of it, he wasn't a powerful and indestructible beast, but a scarred, good-for-almost-nothing human.

Panting, he staggered to his feet, and the rustling stopped. But whoever—or whatever—had made the sounds was still hiding in the bushes.

"Who's there?" he asked. "Show yourself."

The tiny gasp confirmed what he'd thought all along. There was a person hiding behind all that underbrush.

"Unless you're one of the Thirteen, you have nothing to fear from me."

Another gasp, this one accompanied by the barest hint of a whimper.

"Don't freak out on me, okay?" He wasn't sure why he felt the need to reassure this person he didn't know while his entire family was being hunted, but the scent he'd tracked here? It wasn't evil. Or threatening. If anything, it called to him asking for comfort and protection.

As soon as he stepped around the bush, his jaw dropped.

The woman huddled on the ground was covered in dirt and bloody scratches. She held her shackled hands up in front of her, and a foot-long chain hung from between them. Drawing her knees up, hiding her naked body, she shuddered, and he swore under his breath. Heavy metal cuffs were locked around both ankles as well. Her eyes were clouded over, and she squinted like even the barest hint of moonlight was too much for her.

Despite being battered and bruised, she was beautiful. Long dark hair cascaded over her shoulders, falling all the way to the forest floor, and an intense need to calm and care for this woman reared up inside of him. Was this...? No. It couldn't be.

But even though he wanted to reject the very idea of it, he knew he couldn't.

He'd just met his mate.

SAMEEN

"Don't freak out on me, okay?"

His voice soothed her, even though she couldn't see him. The idea of anyone finding her had kept her almost completely still for hours—that and her inability to see, to stand, to even get to her knees.

Another step closer, and she caught a hint of his scent. She...liked it. He smelled like freedom. Like the forest and fresh air.

"Who are you?" he asked.

If only she could tell him. Or see him. A twig snapped under his foot, and she tried to figure out how close he was. Twenty feet? Less?

"I'm Peter. Peter O'Shay. Are you injured?"

Was she? Sameen wasn't sure. She was bleeding from dozens of cuts and scrapes from the rocks and the thorny vines she'd crawled over to get here. But the rest of her? What did you call being kept underground in the dark for so many years, forbidden from even blinking, that your eyes could no longer see? Or being spelled silent for so long, you didn't know if you remembered how to speak.

She didn't move, too scared to even try, but Peter was still coming closer.

"Do you have a name?"

This, she could answer. In a fashion. The slow nod made her head ache. Now that she was free from the spells that kept her bound and immobile, in some sort of stasis, she'd started to feel hunger again. Thirst.

Sameen had patted all around her hiding spot, hoping for some berries she could trust to eat, but had found nothing.

"So…your name?" Peter asked.

He was close now. Not quite close enough to touch, she thought, but close enough he could see her and the state she was in. Sameen tried to inch back, but her legs felt like they weighed a hundred pounds each.

"It's okay. I'm not going to hurt you. See? No weapons. I'm… uh…sorry about the lack of clothes, but it kind of comes with the territory."

She didn't know what he meant, but she reached up with a trembling hand and touched her eyes, then shook her head slightly.

"Oh, shit. You can't see me? Can't see at all?"

"*No.*"

She mouthed the word, hoping he'd understand. He took another step, rustling the brush only inches away from her. Sameen made a tiny, panicked sound—all she was capable of— and even that burned her throat. Panic welled up inside her, along with the scraps and shreds of the elemental powers the Thirteen had channeled into her over so many years.

"Shhh. You're safe. I'm kneeling half a foot away from you, and I won't touch you unless you want me to." His voice was so soothing, and she imagined he was strong. Solid. For years, she'd had nothing but her own thoughts to comfort her, and sometimes, she'd conjured the idea of a big man, dark hair, dark eyes, stubble… He'd always made her feel safe.

But then her mind would fracture, he'd disappear, and she'd remember that she was never safe—would never be safe again.

"Can you talk?"

"*No.*"

Her hands started to shake, and a hint of fire welled up

inside her. Not enough to escape, but enough to sicken her. Falling onto her side, she retched, and Peter swore quietly, then came close enough the heat of his body warmed her.

"Just breathe. Focus on my voice and breathe. Can I touch your shoulder?"

Sameen couldn't answer. Not when she had to use every bit of energy she had just to keep the pain from overwhelming her. She was shaking, her hands clenched into fists in front of her face, the fire burning inside her chest, making her heart pound so hard, she could hear it.

Her thoughts dulled—as they always did when the elements battled within her. A part of her remained on the rocky ground, but the rest of her retreated deep inside, away from the pain.

Strong fingers gripped her shoulders, yet he was gentle. As were his words. "I won't leave you. I don't know who you are, but there's something about you…I have to keep you safe. I need you to find a way to come back to me, sweetheart. I think…we were supposed to find one another."

The seizure took her, and all Sameen wanted were Peter's arms around her. She tried to turn her head, and thought she might have managed. A little. If she could just see him. Maybe everything would be okay.

Opening her mouth in a silent scream, she prayed he'd understand what she needed. Tears tumbled from her eyes, and her body shook so violently, she feared she'd smack her head into one of the larger rocks.

"Shit. I can't *not* hold you. I won't try anything. Just…fuck it." He scooped her into his arms and cradled her against his chest. Strong. Solid. She'd been right. He tucked her head against the curve of his neck and held her close until she passed out.

CHAPTER TWO

PETER

Something soft brushed his chest, and a sweet scent—vanilla and berries—wrapped around him. His back ached, as did his ass, and he didn't know why. Until he opened his eyes. Dawn was approaching, but the sky was still alight with stars, and in his arms, the woman he'd found injured, naked, and ill hours before shifted slowly away from him.

Her muscles were trembling with the effort, and she stopped after each tiny movement, holding her breath like she was trying to figure out if she'd woken him.

"Don't go," he said softly.

The hoarse little whine stabbed him through the heart, and she scrambled off his lap, skittering on all fours until she collapsed less than two feet away. Her shoulders shook with her quiet sobs.

"Tell me what's wrong." The absurdity of the statement hit him smack in the face even as she swiped at her cheeks and the chain hanging from her wrist cuffs clinked in the quiet of the early morning. "Shit. I'm sorry. Just…don't run away from me. Please. I can help you."

She shook her head, and her black locks fanned out over her shoulders, tangling over her eyes. *"No."*

"No? I can at least get those cuffs off and find you some clothes. Not right this second, but I'm staying just a couple of miles from here. Plus, you have to be starving."

The woman pressed her hands to her side and started rocking back and forth, her breath hissing between her teeth. Pain tightened lines around her eyes, and she mouthed something he couldn't understand.

"This is fucking ridiculous. You're hurt, and I can help." Peter scooped her up, ignoring the lightning bolt of pure agony that shot down his left arm.

"No, no, no…" She tried to push against him, and though she was too weak to free herself, the movement made Peter freeze as he caught sight of the symbol burned into her side. He'd seen it before. On Colin. And Farren.

"The Thirteen marked you." If he thought she could stand on her own, he'd set her down. Or, not, because holding her made him even more certain than he'd been the previous night. This woman was his mate, and though the full moon had passed, his wolf refused to let go. He'd protect her until his last breath—if she let him. "Can they control you?"

She nodded and pointed in the opposite direction of Regulus's mansion.

"They want you to go that way? Right now?" His beast growled and clawed to the surface. If he wasn't careful, he'd lose control and shift with her still in his arms.

Another nod.

"Is that what *you* want?"

The small shake of her head sent relief flooding through him, and he touched his forehead to hers. "I can help. Eli—he's one of the elementals with us—he can work protection spells that can hide you from them."

His mate gasped, and tears tumbled down her cheeks. "N-no." The word was barely there, a whisper at best, and seemed to cause her pain, but he clung to it like it was the first meal he'd eaten in years.

"No? Fuck. I wish you could see my face. I'm not lying to you. He's that powerful. The whole place is warded. You'll be safe there. Protected. By all of us. Six werewolves, a vampire—shit, maybe it's five werewolves and two vampires now. I don't know what's going to happen with Ewan once he transitions. Plus Caitlin and Eli. They're both elementals, though Eli has magic in him..."

With every rambling word, she grew more and more agitated until she hissed and doubled over. The brand, pressed to his bicep, started to burn, and Peter awkwardly sank to his knees, groaning as his leg protested.

"Breathe. They won't take you. I promise. But you have to trust me." He cupped her cheeks and brushed her tears away. "I'm a werewolf, sweetheart. A shitty one who can't run like he used to. If I try to carry you back to the mansion, it'll take too long. I can see how much pain you're in. Liam, though...he's a hell of a lot stronger than I am, and if Eli comes with him...we can hide you and you won't have to hurt anymore."

She nodded, arching her brows in a silent query while her whole body trembled. Hope.

"I have to shift. They'll hear me if I shift and call to them. But you have to fight. My wolf can't exactly wrap his arms around you and hold you in place."

Banding her arms around her knees tightly, she lowered her head, making herself as small as possible. Fuck. Peter could see every one of her ribs, along with dozens of long-healed scars. Before he reached for his wolf, he skimmed his hand down her back, and she leaned into him.

"I won't be more than a foot away from you. Not until you can hear my voice again."

SAMEEN

She shouldn't trust him. At best, she'd get him killed. At worst… she didn't want to think of what the Thirteen would do to a werewolf who got between them and their precious conduit. God, she hated that word. She was a person. She'd *been* a person once. She thought. Until they'd reduced her to nothing but a vessel to store all the fragments of the elements they'd collected over the years.

Next to her, leaves rustled, and then she heard the distinct sound of bones breaking. Peter groaned, a long, low sound that turned into a growl as the seconds passed. When all she could hear was panting, she reached for him, needing something to hold on to as the sigil burned into her skin felt like it was twisting and turning, urging her away from this man who'd promised to protect her.

She found soft, thick fur. His neck. Strong, corded muscles. A wet nose swiped her shoulder, and he pressed his big body against her and let out a series of barks and howls. Two minutes later, another wolf answered him from somewhere far away. After another few sounds she couldn't interpret, Peter lay down and started to tremble. Bones broke, and under her hands, his fur disappeared until all she could feel was his skin.

"Still with me?" Peter said, his voice hoarse. "They're coming."

Sameen fumbled for his hand. Though she could barely focus her thoughts with the Thirteen's magic threatening to take over, she traced six letters on his palm.

"Is that your name?" he asked, wrapping his arm around her

and holding her close. "Sameen?"

Her whole body went rigid right as she started to nod, the urge to fight her way free almost overwhelming. She didn't want to go. Didn't want to leave this man who seemed to want to help her. He hadn't hurt her. Not once. He hadn't even hesitated when she'd had the seizure. Just held her and protected her for hours.

A gust of wind ruffled her hair, and Peter's free hand cupped the back of her head. "It's going to get loud and probably a little confusing in a minute, Sameen. Trust me, and I'll protect you."

More than anything, she wished she could put her arms around him, but her wrists were still shackled, and if he let go of her, she was terrified she'd never find him again.

"Who the bloody hell is that?" The deep voice held a faint accent, and Sameen tried to burrow even closer to Peter.

"Someone who needs our help, Eli," Peter growled, and another wolf barked, decidedly angry. "If you think I'd put the pack in danger—either pack—you're a fucking idiot, Liam. The Thirteen *branded* her and whatever spell they used on Fergus and Colin, the one they tried to use on Farren…they're trying to take her. Right now."

"Who is she?" the man—Eli, she thought—asked.

"Sameen. That's all I know. Except…" He buried his nose in her hair, and Eli swore under his breath. Why? She hadn't heard Peter say anything else, but the wolf he'd called Liam made a questioning sound. "Yes," Peter snapped. "I'm sure. She's in pain, Eli. Do something."

All around her, the wind howled. Rain pelted her cheeks, and the ground under them shook, gently at first, then almost violently. When flames started to crackle close by, she whimpered softly, and Peter stroked her back. "It's all part of the casting he does. It's like…this halo of light he holds in his hands."

Peter's voice took on a hint of wonder, and Sameen wished

she could see. She didn't much care about the light beyond whatever it could do to shield her from the Thirteen, but she wanted to know what her protector looked like.

"This is going to feel strange," Peter whispered in her ear. "Like someone just gave you a shot of adrenaline. I won't let go."

She sensed the heat approaching, and the brand on her side throbbed with such intensity, she thought Peter might be able to feel it. The jolt shocked her, despite his warning, but after the moment of intense pain, she could breathe again.

The absence of the Thirteen's compulsion, of the sickening feeling of magic winding its way around her soul and into her mind left her reeling, and she collapsed against Peter's chest, fresh tears streaming down her cheeks.

"You're crying. Shit. Tell me it worked," Peter said.

She couldn't remember the last time she'd smiled. Her lips and cheeks felt strange. Like her body had actually *forgotten* how to be happy, even for a moment. But when Peter blew out a relieved breath, Sameen figured she must have gotten it right. Exhaustion threatened to drag her under, and when Peter smoothed his hand over her hair and nuzzled her neck, she let herself give in to sleep.

PETER

It killed him to let Liam carry Sameen back to the mansion. But when he'd tried to stand with her in his arms, his leg had buckled, and he'd almost dropped her.

At least she'd passed out or fallen asleep before the beta wolf had picked her up, and she didn't stir when he brought her up to the bedroom Peter had claimed as his and laid her in the four-poster bed.

"Who in the feckin' hell is this?" Farren asked from the

doorway as Peter yanked on a pair of jeans and a t-shirt. When she took a step closer, her eyes narrowed, and she pressed her hand to her side. "She's branded. Are all of ya' daft? She—"

"She's mine," Peter growled. "I need Regulus. He's the only one strong enough to break these cuffs off her."

"Yers...fuck me. If Tierney finds his mate in the next week, this entire world's gone batshit sideways. And Regulus went to ground an hour ago. Said he'd be almost impossible to wake until sundown."

"I can help." Caitlin stood just behind Farren with a small velvet bag in her hand. "Liam told me she was injured. I brought some healin' crystals, but I can handle the locks too."

"How?"

"My air." Caitlin's cheeks pinked. "A key is just a way to move the lock tumblers around in a specific pattern. Any teenage air elemental with half a brain learns how."

Peter moved aside, despite his wolf's protests, and let Caitlin ease a hip onto the bed. She lifted one of Sameen's hands and fluttered her fingers over the keyhole. In under a minute, the cuff popped open.

"Shit. That's—"

"Handy? It is." Once she'd finished, Caitlin thrust the manacles at Farren. "Get rid of these. I can smell the magic on them. Maybe Eli can bury them?"

"We'll do it. Do ya' need anythin' else?" Farren asked. "I feel like a rubbish alpha at the moment with Tierney retrievin' the book and all yer notes from Doolin and Ewan..."

"Be with yer mate. The two of ya' need time alone." Caitlin offered Farren a weak smile. "It's been all of twenty-four hours."

"Doesn't feel right with Cade hurtin' like he is." The only female alpha in the world—that Peter knew of—didn't look like she wanted the mantle any longer. Though the two of them had butted heads when he'd arrived in Ireland eight weeks ago, that had been *his* failing. Not hers. She was a good alpha. As good as

Cade, if not better. Cade had lost himself with Mara gone, though now that Peter was only a few feet away from his own mate, he understood.

"Do ya' want help with her?" Caitlin asked. Holding a smoky quartz crystal in her hand, she traced a sigil in the air over Sameen's forehead, another at her heart, and a third all around the brand on her side.

"Help?" He had no fucking clue what he was supposed to *do* with her now. Or even if she were asleep or unconscious.

"Peter." Caitlin's voice held both patience and exasperation.

They'd never gotten along. When she'd shown up in Seattle months after the woman she used to be had helped Mara's sister trap Cade as his wolf and torture him, then kidnap Mara to get back at Cade, Peter had been certain her intentions were anything but noble. He'd been so very wrong, and after Caitlin had risked her life to save Liam from a deranged earth elemental, he'd tried to repair the damage he'd done. But he was pretty sure he'd failed miserably.

"She's been starved, branded, and from the looks of those manacles, a prisoner for years. I count at least six cuts that'll fester if they're not cleaned, and she'll need clothes." Caitlin snagged a blanket from the foot of the bed and tucked it around his mate. "There's probably a first aid kit in the bathroom. I can check the closets for a few items that will fit her. Regulus seems to have entertained some female guests over the years. Some even in the last century."

Peter stared down at the floor, hating that he knew so little about what his own mate needed. "Clothes would be good. And tea? I don't know what she'll be able to eat. Or what she likes."

Caitlin gave him a little nod of approval and left him alone with his mate. His naked, injured, blind mate.

First aid kit. He could handle that. Maybe.

IT WAS ALMOST noon before she stirred. Peter had cleaned her wounds, and Caitlin had brought an armful of clothes, an electric kettle and tea service on a tray, some crackers, and a candy bar. Before Tierney had left for Doolin, he'd taken one of the many cars Regulus kept in his underground garage and bought them enough food for a small army. All the vampire kept in the house was blood. Unsurprising.

Peter had tried to sit in the chair in the corner of the room for a bit, but he couldn't stand being that far away from Sameen, so eventually, he'd stretched out on the bed with his back against the headboard—as close to the edge as he could be to give her space.

He must have nodded off, because he woke to her ragged breathing. "Sameen? You're safe. Don't panic, please."

"Peter." If he hadn't been staring right at her lips, he wouldn't have caught the word. Or her wince of pain and hard swallow.

"I'm right here. This house is warded, and no one's going to find you here."

She reached for him, only then seeming to realize her hands were free. The gasp, the way her mouth formed a little *o*, and the tears gathering in the corners of her eyes hit him hard, and he slid an arm around her shoulders to help her sit up.

The blanket fell away, but she was so intent on touching her now bare wrists, he didn't think she noticed. Peter and his wolf were acutely aware of her naked body, however, and he quickly lifted the blanket and tucked it under her arms. Only then did her cheeks flush a shade darker.

"There's a tea kettle. I could make you some. For your throat. And Caitlin—that's Liam's mate—found some clothes that should fit you. Or, I could run some hot water in the tub. Or food? Or—fuck."

His mate looked completely overwhelmed, and he kicked himself for throwing so many things at her at once.

"Tea first. Okay?" he asked.

After a minute, she nodded, then curled on her side with the blanket pulled up to her neck. He'd kept the lights dim on purpose, not sure if her eyes were sensitive, but she squeezed them shut anyway and buried her face in the pillow.

Caitlin had suggested adding a splash of whiskey and a generous amount of honey and lemon to the cup—her mother's favorite remedy for a sore throat—and Peter did so, then returned to the bed, helped her sit up and lean against his chest, and steadied the mug.

She almost choked on the first sip. Dammit. He should have warned her. But she took a second, and a third sip, and almost smiled. "Where," she whispered, "is...here?" This time, the words didn't seem to cause her as much pain.

"Scotland. Not far from Glasgow. Is the tea all right?" He sounded like an idiot. Like he had no idea how to care for a woman—or for anyone. He certainly had no idea how to talk to her. He had a thousand questions, but he'd already gone overboard once and all he was trying to do was figure out what she most needed.

"Uh huh." When she gave up after another few sips, he wanted to kick something. Preferably his own ass. He'd obviously fucked it all up.

"I can call Caitlin. She's better at tea—"

Sameen shook her head. "Too long...need to go slow..."

"Too long?" He set the cup on the nightstand and balled his hands into fists. "I can't stand not knowing what to do for you."

Her flinch riled his wolf. The beast wasn't angry at her, but at himself for being such a fucking idiot he'd scared her when what she probably needed most of all was to feel safe.

"I'll be right back," he said, his voice taking on a harsh edge. "I need a minute. Just a minute." Running away from her felt like the worst decision of his life, but if he couldn't put some space between them, he'd screw up even more.

CHAPTER THREE

*T*he door shut, and she might as well have been locked back in the Thirteen's dungeon for how very alone she felt.

It didn't matter that she was free from their chains and spells. She was still in an unfamiliar room, blind save for diffuse shadows—all her damaged eyes could process—and too weak to do more than sit up.

"Peter?" Barely a whisper. She hated feeling so helpless. Years had passed since she'd had to concern herself with complicated thoughts. Or...*any* thoughts, really, beyond praying for death or wondering if they'd come for her soon, make her suffer more than the endless days, weeks, and months locked inside her own body.

Sometimes, she remembered her last day of freedom. It had been warm. The scent of lilies hanging heavy in the gardens outside her apartment. That was all she had left. She couldn't picture her bedroom. Her kitchen. Friends, family...

Until Peter had tucked the blanket around her, she hadn't even thought of her own nakedness. What did she need clothing for? Her entire purpose was to absorb as much elemental power as the Thirteen could channel into her and then *die* transforming it into some mythical *spirit* element she was certain she'd never be able to conjure no matter how much they tortured her.

Fear snaked along her spine, curling around her heart. What if he didn't come back? Or worse. What if this was all just a figment of her broken mind?

Slowly, she wriggled until her toes brushed thick carpeting. The bed was tall, but if she braced herself, she might be able to stand. The door hadn't sounded that far away. Six or seven steps? She'd crawled, inches at a time, to put distance between her and the dungeon. She could do this.

The blanket was another challenge, but after several tries, she had it wrapped around her in such a way that she had a free hand to hold out in front of her in case there were obstacles she couldn't see.

At what was barely a shuffle, Sameen crept forward, and just as her legs started to shake, she found a wall. Then wood. A handle. It turned easily, but then the door swung inwards with such force, she stumbled back and collapsed in a heap.

"Fuck!" Peter landed on top of her, and she yelped, though it sounded more like a weak grunt than anything else. "Sameen. Did I hurt you?"

She'd expected anger, but instead, he rolled to the side, wrapped an arm around her waist, and then ran his nose along the curve of her neck. The intimate gesture made her heart beat a little faster, and she thought she could almost sense his worry.

"N-no. Scared..." How could she explain her ridiculous fears? No normal person would think a comfortable bed and a soft blanket were figments of their imagination.

"Shit, sweetheart. I'm sorry." With a groan, he helped her to her feet. Had she hurt him? If so, she wasn't sure she could forgive herself. "I shouldn't have left you. I'm not...good with people."

She hadn't thought of herself as anything but the Thirteen's conduit in so long, she couldn't remember what it had been like to be Sameen. To be a person. Her throat tightened up, but Peter sounded so shattered, she wasn't going to let a little discomfort stop her from talking now that she finally *could*.

"You were good with me."

He let out a snort as he helped her back to the bed. "If that were true, you'd never be scared again." When he'd propped her against a pillow, he cupped her cheek. "You look worse than when I found you. What do you need? Food?"

Her stomach was hollow, and she couldn't remember the last time she'd eaten.

"Caitlin brought up crackers and a chocolate bar. The good kind we can't get back home."

The wrapper crinkled before he pressed the treat into her hand. *Oh, God.* If she weren't careful, she'd eat the whole thing and end up sick.

"Home?" she asked through a bite of cherries and creamy goodness she'd forgotten existed in the world.

"Seattle." Peter sat close enough his warmth comforted her—and also made her realize just how good he smelled. Like the outdoors. Clean and fresh and not at all like magic. "Where's your home?" he asked.

His voice took on an odd timber, like he didn't want to know. Or maybe he was only concerned about her having to talk.

"I lived in..." The chocolate bar tumbled from her fingers, and her throat tightened, panic raising goosebumps on her arms. "I don't know."

Peter wrapped her in a gentle embrace. "It's okay. You'll

remember. And...if you don't, you'll always have a home here. If you want. With me."

PETER

Get a hold of yourself, asshole. She's obviously been abused, chained up only God knows where for so long she doesn't know which way is up, and you were about to tell her you're her mate?

Either she'd already figured that out, or she hadn't understood him, because she let him hold her until her breathing settled. He had so many questions, but if he kept pressing her for answers, he was afraid she'd shut down on him completely.

"Want more?" he asked, retrieving the chocolate.

Sameen shook her head, and shit. He could feel the sadness and despair emanating from her in waves.

"Talk to me. Or...would writing be easier? I don't know what to do for you." Tipping her head up, he waited for her to open her eyes. Even if she couldn't see him, he wanted to know what had happened to blind her. Her irises were cloudy, the whites bloodshot. Gently, he skimmed his finger just under her right eye. "Did *they* do this?"

"Trapped me in my own body." She spoke slowly. Carefully. Like she was testing each word. Whether to figure out if it would hurt or because she was afraid she'd say something wrong, he wasn't sure. "Couldn't move. Couldn't blink. But awake. Always awake."

"Fuck. Sameen, how did you not go insane?"

Her huff might have been a laugh. "Think I did. Not blinking...is like your eyes are on fire."

"Who did this? Which one of them?" His voice took on a hard, rough edge, his wolf demanding vengeance for the torture his mate had suffered. If it was his last act on earth, he'd disembowel the practitioner who caused her such pain.

"Celia. She leads them." With a shudder, she rubbed her throat. "Hurts. Tea?"

Shit. She shouldn't have to ask. Not for anything. Caitlin should have stayed. She'd know what to do. How to take care of Sameen. "Let me make you a fresh cup. We have more food. Tierney bought enough to feed half of Scotland. Or I can go out and get you something. McDonald's? Glasgow's only twenty minutes away."

"Don't go!" She grabbed his arm, holding on like her life depended on him staying by her side. God, he was an idiot. She hadn't wanted him to leave the *room*. And here he'd suggested leaving the house?

Softening his voice, he rested his hand over hers. "I won't go anywhere unless you ask me to. I promise." The relief spreading across her delicate features gave him hope that maybe she wouldn't reject him when he finally worked up the courage to tell her they were mates. "I'll just get that tea."

MARA

She woke in the same position she'd fallen asleep in, her muscles stiff, her arms wrapped around her belly in the dim light. How long had she been here? Her baby kicked, the tiny impact against her palm bringing tears to her eyes. "I'm so sorry," she whispered.

It wasn't until she sat up that she realized how much bigger she was. Another week, at least. And so very hungry.

Footsteps scuffed against stone, and she hastily swiped at her tears. She wouldn't let them see her cry.

The bars parted, and a woman dressed in a light purple robe set a tray down in front of her. "You have one hour to eat."

"Wait," Mara called as the woman returned to the corridor and the bars closed back up again. "I need more than that. Sunlight. Fresh air. Exercise. You want this baby to be healthy? You have to let me out of here."

Pushing back her hood to reveal spiked blond hair and a face that couldn't be older than twenty-five, the practitioner glared at Mara. "You do not get to make demands of us, elemental. You will obey. Or you will suffer."

"My name is Mara, bitch. The least you could do is use it."

"Eat." Drawing the single word out, the woman pointed at the tray and her eyes glowed a lighter purple.

Mara fought not to pick up the spoon, but the mark on her side burned, and her fingers had a mind of their own. The practitioner didn't move until half the stew was gone, and Mara thought she was going to be sick.

"Please," she managed between bites of some of the most overcooked spinach she'd ever seen. "Let me stop."

With a sigh, the woman blinked, and her eyes darkened again. The spoon clattered to the floor, and Mara sank back against the wall. "One hour, elemental. Then the lights go out."

The cell around her started to spin, and her vision shrank down to a single pinprick of light. Her fire element had taken control, and it was pissed.

"Dammit. You can't keep doing that without any warning!" Mara screamed silently from the small box her other half had forced her into.

"Yes. I can."

"Oh, so we can talk now. Any bright ideas?"

Only silence answered her, and she had to watch herself finish the stew, slowly.

"If we can't get out of here, they're going to take our baby."

The word *our* seemed to have an impact, because the glass of milk wobbled in her hand.

"You're obviously stronger than I am since you can take over at any time. Call fire to you. See if you can fight their magic."

How long had it been? At least thirty minutes. Once the milk and water were gone, Mara's hand lifted, and she could feel the power surge up inside of her. But then the mark flared, and she cried out, the pain making her double over. Her palm wasn't even warm.

Nausea clawed its way up her throat, and she scrambled on hands and knees all the way to the toilet.

The baby needed that food. If she were advancing a week every time they forced her to sleep, her daughter would end up malnourished if she didn't keep the food down. Unless...maybe that was it. They hadn't told her not to throw up. They'd just commanded her to eat.

"Do it. Come on. If you're any part of Katerina...if you came from her or if you are her, think like her. Stick your finger down your throat—my throat—and throw up. Everything they just made us eat."

With a pained cry that sounded almost like a growl, Katerina —that was all Mara could think of to call this other part of her —jammed a finger down Mara's throat.

God, she hated throwing up. The endless morning sickness had made her cry more than once, and Mara wasn't a crier. Not before she'd gotten pregnant anyway. But now, she welcomed the disgusting sensation.

"Just hang on, Rachel," she told her daughter. *"It's probably going to get worse before it gets better. But we're going to find a way out of here."*

TEN MINUTES LATER, her stomach empty and her fiery hitch-hiker back in hiding, Mara hoped she hadn't made a terrible mistake.

"Get up." Celia's order echoed from halfway down the corridor, and Mara rose on unsteady legs, unable to resist the practitioner's command. "Consider this your only warning, elemental. Try something like that again, and you will regret it."

"I need fresh air," Mara said softly. "Just for a few minutes. I know I can't fight you." She gingerly touched her side where the sigil still burned. "I don't want to feel that pain ever again. I just want to know my baby will be safe. That she'll be healthy. And," she sniffled and swiped at her nose, "I don't want to die without ever seeing the sun again. Can you understand that?"

"We studied you before we knew your child would be strong enough to create the last element. You are intelligent, yet you take us for fools. I will not let you out of this cell until you are ready to give birth. Ask again, and I will hunt down your mate just so he can watch you die."

"No! Leave Cade alone. Please!" She lunged for the bars and managed to get one hand through to grab Celia's arm. "Don't hurt him."

"Accept your fate, elemental. And obey." Celia's lips curved into a gleeful smile. "Lie down now. Wouldn't want you falling when the lights go out."

All the fight left her like someone had stuck a pin in a balloon. She would die, the Thirteen would take her daughter, and she'd never see Cade again. There were no tears. No sadness or outrage. Only resignation. Her life was over.

Darkness surrounded her. The other consciousness locked deep inside screamed at her to fight, but Mara didn't want to listen. All she wanted to do was sleep.

CHAPTER FOUR

LIVIE

"Where is he?" Livie demanded as she strode into the mansion. When every one of the pack stopped answering their cell phones thirty-six hours ago, Livie had spent twenty minutes snuggling Serena, then headed straight for the airport. She'd broken all kinds of speed records driving to Doolin, and finding Farren's house deserted and with the back wall half-destroyed had set her off, and she'd been yelling at Shawn over video when Tierney had shown up.

"Livie?" Caitlin ran out of a massive living room with vaulted ceilings and dark tapestries on the walls. "Ya' came?"

"Of course I did. Mara's missing and Cade's not answering my calls. You expected me to stay in fucking Canada?" She dropped her duffel bag on the fancy tile floor so she could hug Caitlin. "You've lost weight. Too much. Where's everyone else?"

"Liam's patrollin'. Farren and Eli are in their room. Regulus is waitin' for Ewan to transition, and Peter's...with his mate."

"The hell? Where did Peter find a mate in all of this? And

when?" If she'd walked in to a vampire orgy, she'd be less surprised. "If he was distracted fighting the Thirteen, I'm going to kick his ass."

"He wasn't," Caitlin assured her.

Tierney nudged the front door shut behind her and headed for the living room with a rolling suitcase. "Did ya' say Peter found his *mate*? What the feckin' hell is in the water around here? I was gone for all of ten hours."

"She was branded by the Thirteen." Caitlin ran a hand through her reddish brown locks. "When Peter found her, she was a mile away from the compound we hit. Livie, her wrists and ankles were chained, she can't see, and I'm not even sure she can talk. I don't think she's a threat, but she does need our protection."

Rolling her eyes, Livie muttered, "We'll see about that. Have you told Cade?"

Caitlin snorted. "He won't talk to any of us. Threatened to start runnin' and not stop until he caught her scent. Regulus has a full gym in the east wing basement, and Cade's been down there punchin' everythin' in sight until he passes out from exhaustion. Then wakes up and starts all over again. It's good this place is so well insulated. We've been takin' turns bringin' food to him. Not that he's eaten anythin'.'"

"I'm going down there to see if I can yank his head out of his ass. We need our alpha back so we can find Mara. And when I'm done, I want to talk to this new 'mate' of Peter's. I should have been with you all from the beginning. It's my job to manage the security for this pack, and since the pup was born, I've been shirking my duties. Maternity leave's over."

CAITLIN HADN'T BEEN KIDDING. The large open space at the bottom of a long flight of stairs had everything. A treadmill, a huge rack of free weights larger than any she'd ever seen, a steam room, jacuzzi tub, and three separate heavy bags lined up not too far from the left wall. A fourth had been destroyed, now nothing but a pile of sand on the floor next to ripped leather swinging from a chain overhead.

Sitting in the darkest corner, naked, with his arms around his knees and his head bowed, was her alpha.

Livie marched over to him, barely pausing to grab a black terry cloth robe draped over one of the weight benches. Balling it up, she threw it at him. "Bossman, get up. Now."

He growled, his wolf flashing in his ice blue eyes, until he focused on her. "Livie? Is that really you?"

"No. A figment of your imagination just hit you in the head with a bathrobe." She rolled her eyes. "Of course it's me. Did you expect me to just sit in that fucking apartment in Vancouver doing *nothing* after my alpha's mate—my *sister* in every way that counts—was taken? Because if you did, you're a lot further gone than I thought."

Cade flinched at the word "mate" and dropped his head into his hands. "I've lost her. I can't feel her anymore. She could already be dead and I wouldn't know."

"If *I* were one of the most powerful group of witches in existence and didn't have a way to hide my kidnapping victims, I'd be pretty damn ashamed of myself," Livie said sharply. "Now put on that robe and come upstairs. Peter apparently found a mate during all this fuckery. According to Caitlin, the Thirteen branded her, chained her up somewhere, and probably tortured her. I'd say the chances of her knowing *something* that can help us find Mara are pretty high."

After a beat, when he didn't react to anything she'd said, Livie stomped closer and let her wolf rise to the surface. Her blue eyes burned so bright, she swore the dark little corner lit up, and when she growled at Cade, she did it with enough anger that any self-respecting alpha would react on instinct to put her in her place.

But Cade just sat there, not looking at her, his muscles rigid, his hands bloodied and bruised from what she imagined had been almost thirty-six hours of pure rage and despair.

So she sank down next to him and put her arm around his shoulders. He flinched and tried to pull away, but she caught the hitch in his breath. "You've known me since I was sixteen, boss-man. Seen me at my best. And my worst. Hell, you half raised me. And I understand. What you're feeling? Serena's the best fucking thing that's ever happened to me, with Shawn a close second." She leaned her head a little closer and lowered her voice. "I'd say don't tell him to spare his ego, but he feels the same way."

Nothing. Not even a huff at her mate's expense.

"You have to come back, Cade. We need you. *Mara* needs you."

Whether it was her use of his first name—something she *never* did, though she couldn't say why—or hearing her say "Mara," her words finally sunk in, and Cade started shaking. First a highly controlled tremble, then almost violent, body-wracking sobs.

"Let it out, bossman," she said quietly. "We'll find her. Or we'll all die trying."

<hr>

PETER

The quiet knock roused him, but thankfully, Sameen didn't stir. She'd managed another half cup of tea and a few crackers, but she'd been so upset after telling him how she lost her sight, she'd practically passed out as soon as he'd tucked her back into bed and wrapped his arms around her.

His mate trusted him. That alone was a miracle after all she'd been through. But it was more than that. She curled against him, almost desperate in the way she held onto his hands. He'd found some eye ointment in the first aid kit that promised to soothe irritation and corneal abrasions, and he'd carefully tipped her head back and applied a line to each of her lower lids before she slept. Maybe it would help? They needed Christine. The pack's healer was still in Seattle, and more than once Peter thought about calling her.

"Peter?" Caitlin whispered as she poked her head in. "Livie's here. Downstairs with Cade. It's almost sundown. Regulus should be above ground in an hour or so."

He glanced at his mate, her face relaxed in a way he hadn't seen since he'd discovered her naked and terrified, hiding behind a bush. "You need to know what happened to Sameen."

"Has she told ya' anythin'?" Another door in the mansion slammed, and the noise startled Sameen awake.

"Peter? Who's here?" she asked, tensing.

"Just Caitlin. It's all right." He helped her sit up, and she blinked hard as she turned towards the door. "I'm sorry, sweetheart. There's so much I need to tell you still, but we're out of time."

"Time? Are you...leaving?" Her voice was so much stronger than it had been earlier, and it did things to him he wasn't prepared for. Like made his cock press painfully against the zipper of his jeans.

"No," he growled. Fuck. He had to get himself under control. His mate didn't deserve any of this. Not his bad temper, not his inability to see to her needs, and definitely not her position as some pawn in the Thirteen's deadly games. He looked to Caitlin for help, and the air elemental cleared her throat.

"Sameen? I think you met Liam—or Liam's wolf—early this mornin'? I'm his mate. We need yer help. Everythin' ya' can tell us about the Thirteen and how to find them. It's close to nightfall, and the vampire helping us wants to go back to the compound we destroyed to see if we can find any other clues about where they might have taken Mara. She's our alpha's mate, and she's pregnant. Ye're the only one who's seen the Thirteen—who's spoken to them—in decades besides Regulus."

Peter tightened his embrace when Sameen sucked in a sharp breath.

"They never let me speak." She touched her throat, gently, and shook her head. "I never saw anything beyond the first cell they locked me in. After that...my eyes...I couldn't see anything else."

Caitlin frowned, falling silent for so long, Sameen started to fidget with the blanket she clutched to her chest and Peter called Caitlin's name.

"Somethin' one of the practitioners said when we were in the dungeon. I had to use a compulsion charm on her." With a shudder, Caitlin continued. "They're vile, but damn hard to fight—even for a witch." Starting to pace, she ran a hand through her hair. "I kept askin' her where Mara was and how we could find her, and right before she...died—I think she took her own life rather than let us kill her—she said, 'The voice of one who cannot speak and the sight of one who has never seen will find the blood of the stone. Without those, ye're doomed to fail, and the elemental will be ours forever.'"

"You think Sameen's the one who can't speak and hasn't seen?" Peter asked.

"If the prophecy fits," Farren said from the doorway.

Sameen swiveled her head between Peter and Caitlin, panic stiffening her muscles. "Peter? Is that someone else?"

"Farren. She's alpha of the Doolin pack." He straightened his shoulders, letting his wolf rise to the surface where he knew the beast would flare in his eyes. "Are we having a fucking party in here? You realize Sameen can't see you, right? Maybe knock first? Or at least don't all come barging into my bedroom unannounced?"

"My own room's right across the hall, ya' arse. I heard what Caitlin said. If this woman is truly yer mate, she's goin' to have to get used to—"

"M-mate?" Sameen asked. "What is she talking about?"

Peter's wolf railed against the man's hold, and he was so angry, he was half tempted to let the beast free to scare the fuck out of Farren. Except she was stronger than he was by half or more, and she'd probably kick his ass. And then where would he be? So he settled for letting the wolf glow in his eyes and turn his voice into a growl. "Get. Out. Now!"

Caitlin ushered Farren from the room and shut the door behind her, but the damage had already been done.

Sameen shoved against Peter's chest until he released her and scrambled out of bed, her legs unsteady. "What did she mean?"

"Last night, when I told you I thought we were meant to find one another?" He held up his hands as he approached, then realized she couldn't see his body language, his eyes, the fear he knew had to be written all over his face. "Sameen, werewolves don't fall in love like humans do. Mating is based on instinct. The first time I touched you, before you could talk, before I knew anything about you, I knew you were...*mine*."

"I'm not *yours!*" she cried. "I don't even know who I am, Peter. How can I possibly be *yours?*"

"Fuck. That was the wrong thing to say. Or the wrong way to say it." He took a step closer. "Take my hand. Please."

"No." Her voice cracked, and she hugged herself tightly, wavering on her feet like she was about to fall over.

Peter skimmed his fingertips along her arm, and her lower lip wobbled. "Nothing happens between us unless you want it to, Sameen. I promise."

"I don't know what that means," she whispered.

Folding her into his embrace, Peter ran his nose along the curve of her neck. Shit. She felt so good in his arms. And when she wasn't panicked, he could sense the trust she'd put in him. There was no fucking way he'd violate that, but he had to let her know what she meant to him—even after less than a day.

"My wolf knows we're meant to be together. But he's not in charge. I am. I'll take care of you—as much as you let me—but if anything makes you uncomfortable, just say the word."

"Everything makes me uncomfortable. It's all...new to me. Just being able to move of my own free will." She peered up at him, and in the dimly-lit room, squinted and furrowed her brow. "Is your hair...black?"

"Can you see it?" Cupping her cheek, he checked her eyes, and fuck if they didn't look slightly clearer. "Come into the bathroom with me. The light's better in there."

She didn't hesitate when he wrapped an arm around her waist and guided her across the room.

"Ten steps," she whispered when he took her hand and placed it on the edge of the countertop. "Three more from the bed."

"I'm going to turn the light on now." Peter shielded her eyes with one hand and flipped the switch with the other. Sameen sucked in a sharp breath, and after a few seconds, Peter lowered his arm. "Look at me?"

Under the milky scarring, he thought he saw a hint of brown, and she blinked rapidly. "I can't *see*. Not like I want to. But maybe...a little color. Dark brown or black hair?" Sameen reached up and touched his messy locks. "You're pale. Like...really pale. And I'm...I'm not."

She sounded so confused, and Peter didn't understand why until she brushed her fingers over her own hair. It fell all the way to her hips in gentle, but tangled waves, and she followed the length, letting it slip through her fingers as tears gathered in her eyes.

"You...don't remember what you look like?"

The slow shake of her head was overshadowed by the body-wracking sobs she desperately tried to hold in.

"Sameen. Breathe. I'm right here, and you're safe."

"Who forgets what they look like?" she said, burying her face against his chest. "They took everything from me, Peter. I'm not even a *person* anymore. I don't remember my last name. Where I used to live. What I was studying at university...if I have any family...or had..."

"We'll figure all of that out. I promise. And you *are* a person, Sameen." He turned her so they were both facing the mirror, hoping she could make out some semblance of what they looked like together. "Your hair is like the night sky with no stars. Inky black, and I bet it shines when it's clean. Your skin is a deep tawny. You're shorter than Farren, a bit taller than Caitlin. But you're the perfect height for me to do this." Leaning down, Peter ran his nose along her neck.

She shuddered, and he caught the slightest hint of her arousal.

Too soon, asshole. Back it off.

"Why did you do that?" she asked, her voice dropping to a whisper.

"It's instinctual. I don't understand it myself. Is it...okay?" Peter wasn't sure what he'd do if Sameen told him to stop. Besides back away and see if Regulus had another home gym where he could beat the shit out of something.

"It makes me feel safe."

He wasn't sure if he'd ever heard sweeter words. "You *are* safe with me, Sameen. I promise."

CHAPTER FIVE

SAMEEN

Her mate? This man she'd never seen, who'd found her unable to speak or protect herself, who'd not only stopped the Thirteen from taking her, but had cared for her, comforted her, and made her feel like a human being again...was her mate?

The Thirteen had spoken of mating around her before. After a few years, they'd stopped thinking of her as a person. Of course, so had she. They'd talked freely. Of their plans. Of the elementals who'd foiled them. Of what they wanted to do once they'd harnessed the power of spirit.

Sameen was still wearing nothing but the blanket wrapped around her, and she could feel the dirt and sap stuck to her body every time she moved. Peter had drawn her a bath, guided her over to the tub, and had made sure she knew exactly where the soap and towels were before leaving her alone—but not too alone.

She could hear him moving around in the bedroom, and a

part of her wished she'd been strong enough to ask him to join her. Or help her. Despite not knowing him—not knowing a lot of things—she trusted him more than she trusted herself right now. And she was attracted to him. When he held her or said her name, something warmed in her core.

Easing herself into the water, she sighed as her muscles started to loosen. The Thirteen had taken so much from her. Freedom. Memories. Her very identity. But what she wanted most of all at the moment? Her sight.

Maybe if she could see her own face, she'd remember who she'd been.

Anxiety curled around her heart as she ran her hands over her body. Had her breasts always been so small? Her stomach so hollow? She didn't think so. Touching the brand on her side brought a flash of memory. Screaming. The scent of burning flesh. Hers.

Then dread. Because they'd told her what they were about to do. One of the few times any of the Thirteen had actually spoken *to* her.

"No! Please! You can't do this. I'm a person. Not your property."

"You are what we say you are," Celia replied. *"A conduit. Nothing more. You will not speak, you will not fight us, and you will obey our every command."*

Sameen almost called out for Peter as Celia's words echoed in her mind. The feeling of helplessness that had overtaken her in that moment...it was like she'd died chained to their altar. Whoever she'd been...that woman was gone.

Stop it. You're free now. You can be someone new.

Did she even want to be someone new? As she worked the knots out of her long hair, she tried to imagine who she'd even care to be.

Strong. Unafraid. Bold.

She was none of those things. Not after everything they'd done to her.

The simple act of running the washcloth over her cheeks made her feel more human, and when the water started to cool, she fumbled for the drain plug, wrapped herself in a towel, and carefully made her way to the door. "Peter?"

"Right here." He was at her side before her feet touched the thick rug. "I spread the clothes out on the bed. Take my hand?"

Bras and panties on the left. T-shirts next. A pair of jeans. Two pairs of what he called "yoga pants." Socks. Sweaters.

"I'll turn around. But if you need help..."

Sameen stopped him, confused. "You've already seen me naked."

"You didn't have a choice then. You do now."

Choice. He thought to give her a choice? Her entire life had been taken from her, and Peter was giving it back to her piece by piece. There was so much she wanted to say to him, but in a few minutes, she'd have to talk to the rest of his pack, and she wasn't sure how long her voice would hold this time, so she just nodded and waited for his shadowy, hazy form to move a few feet away.

The bra proved difficult, but she managed it after three tries. With every piece of clothing she picked up, she reclaimed a little more of herself. Until she tugged on a pair of socks. Tears burned her eyes. How could she have forgotten the comfort of a thick, warm pair of socks?

"Okay. Done."

Peter turned around, and when he didn't say a word, Sameen started to fiddle with the hem of the sweater.

"Did I do something wrong?"

"Shit. No." Peter ran his hands down her arms and linked their fingers. "You're gorgeous, Sameen. I was right about your hair. It shines."

Her cheeks flushed hot, and she pressed closer to him. "I'm scared, Peter."

"I won't let anything happen to you." He tucked a lock of hair behind her ear and touched his forehead to hers. "No matter what you decide about us—and I won't pressure you—I'll always protect you. With my life."

FARREN

Eli, Caitlin, and Tierney sat around an imposing dining room table with the book and their various notepads spread out over the dark wood. Farren had written down every single bit of nonsense Paddy had ever said to her, and she hoped once Peter brought his new mate down, they might find some answers.

If the woman truly had been the Thirteen's captive for years, she'd have insight none of the rest of them could ever hope for.

"Farren." Regulus appeared next to her, his refined voice devoid of all emotion. "The boy has woken."

Her heart seized, and across the room, Eli's head snapped up. It only took him a moment to understand what was going on, and he stood.

Waving him off, Farren steeled her face into a mask. She had to do this on her own, even though she was desperate to have her mate at her side. "Did he say anythin'?" she asked as she followed Regulus to the door leading to the basement of the west wing.

"He asked for you." The vampire paused with his hand on the knob. "He is displeased with me."

"I'd be displeased with ya' too." She peered up at Regulus, eyes narrowed. "What do I need to know?"

"He has fed. The scent of wolf blood is not one most of my kind enjoy, but there is no telling how this one will feel given his origins. He is restrained, and he will stay that way until I can determine whether the beast living inside him is also subject to a sire's control."

"That *beast* is subject to *my* control, ya' bastard." Farren wanted to shake the vampire, but if she tried, he could snap her neck before she even saw him move.

"Not at the moment. Perhaps not ever." Regulus smoothed a hand over his shoulder-length black hair, a hint of regret creeping into his tone. "Most newly made vampires vacillate between bouts of self-loathing and self-imposed starvation and ravenous, unbridled hunger. Once they accept who and what they are, they cease to be a danger to those around them, but this process takes time. It is a sire's responsibility to restrain their progeny when they cannot control themselves."

"Ewan won't hurt me." Farren had to believe there was still something left of the boy. Some part of him that still recognized her as his alpha.

"In his human form? No. He will not. My control forbids it. But as a wolf? For all I know of the matter, I will have no control at all." Regulus held Farren's gaze, unblinking, and she barely resisted the urge to shudder at the complete lack of empathy in his eyes. "Do not attempt to release him. The restraints are not comfortable, but he is not in pain. The newly made are often so desperate to end their new existence, they will say and do anything to accomplish the task. Do not be swayed."

"I'm still his alpha."

"Perhaps, but I am his sire. That bond cannot be severed unless he chooses to meet the sun. I can force him to bend to my will in a way you never could. I am afraid, she-wolf, that I outrank you."

"Ye're a feckin' areshole, Regulus."

"I do not disagree with you." The vampire nodded towards the stairs. "He is waiting. I will be close. And yes, I will hear every word you say. As the boy has heard every word we have said."

Farren rubbed her hands on her thighs. "Right, then. Well, let's get on with it."

The basement was deathly silent. Vampires didn't *need* to breathe, strictly speaking, though Regulus had told her most chose to adopt the habit for the comfort of other beings.

As Farren reached the last step, though, a chain rattled. Shite. Ewan was a good man. Sweet. Loyal. With a sense of honor she'd always thought old fashioned. How could she have failed him like this? Let him be turned into a creature who'd forever walk in darkness?

Naked Edison bulbs hung from the ceiling, lending a comforting warm glow to the lavish space. To her left, Farren caught sight of an opulent bedroom with a king-sized bed made up with black sheets, slightly mussed, and a thick Persian rug over the fancy tile floors. Regulus wanted for nothing, and that brought her a small measure of comfort. Ewan would be cared for. At least physically.

Another rattle made Farren turn. "Shite."

The young man stood against a stone wall, silver cuffs binding his wrists at his sides. A meter away, a lavish coffin lay open, deep gouges in the lining of the lid.

"Farren. Get me out of here. Ya' know I'm no threat. That arse won't listen." His voice had taken on a hint of a lisp, and as he continued to struggle, his fangs peeked out, perching on his lower lip.

"I can't, Ewan. Ya' know that. Regulus would be here before I even started, and he's yer sire." Farren shoved her hands into her pockets so Ewan wouldn't see her fingers trembling. His formerly green eyes had turned blood red, and his skin had paled to the color of alabaster.

"And ye're my alpha!" he shouted. "I never wanted to be… this!" The man's eyes shimmered, but rather than tears flowing from the corners, drops of blood trailed down his cheeks. "Please. I just want my life back."

"This *is* yer life now. And it's better than bein' dead, luv. One of Glenna's minions snapped yer neck. I couldn't stop it. I let ya' down so many times over the years, and this...I failed ya'. I'm so very sorry."

"Did ya' ask him to turn me?" The growl was half feral, and Ewan jerked the chains, sending a few bits of stone tumbling from the wall. "Ya' had no right to do that!"

"I did not ask him." Farren stepped closer, lowering her voice and trying for something close to soothing. Not that she'd ever been very good at soothing. "I thought ya' dead until Regulus opened his trunk to show me yer body."

Ewan sagged, his head bowed. "I don't want to live like this, Farren."

Her heart shattered, and she swallowed hard. "Please don't say that. Not yet. Give it a few days. Nights. Let Regulus teach ya' how to be...what ya' are."

"An abomination?" he snarled. "I drank *blood*, Farren. And it was the best feckin' meal I've ever had."

"So? Vampires drink blood. When ya' were bitten, how did ya' feel the first time ya' shifted?"

"Like I wanted to die," he said. "I thought my life was over."

"And it wasn't. Ya' adapted. Ya' discovered how good it felt to run. To be faster and stronger than ya' were before." Ignoring Regulus's warning, Farren rested her hand on Ewan's shoulder. The young man jerked, and she forced herself not to pull away. His skin, which should have been so warm, was now ice cold. "If I'm still yer alpha, then what I say will carry weight, yeah?"

He nodded, and the brokenness, the confusion, and the pain shone in the deep red irises.

"I'm orderin' ya', as yer alpha, to give this new...existence some time. I don't want ya' to suffer, Ewan. But let us see if we can find a way for ya' to accept who ya've become. I won't leave ya'. None of us will."

Bloody tears spilled onto the man's cheeks, and sobs

wracked his chiseled frame. Farren didn't know if her words had done any good, and she was too damn scared to ask. If he said no, she'd have one more failure in her ledger, and could her heart survive the tally?

"How long?" he choked out with his head bowed, his gaze on her boots.

"A week. Ya' will not give up on us or yerself for one full week. After that, if ye're still feelin' like there's no hope, we'll find a way for ya' to die in peace."

"One week." He didn't raise his head, but the acceptance in his tone—even though sharpened by grief and rage, gave her a small spark of hope. And a spark was all she needed to start a fire.

CHAPTER SIX

PETER

He should have insisted that Caitlin find his mate some shoes to wear. Her socks were too slippery for these floors. Sameen held onto his arm, and when they reached the top of the stairs, he took a step before he remembered she couldn't see them.

She yelped softly as her foot found nothing but air, and Peter caught her, hauling her back against him as he went down and landed on his ass. "Shit. I'm sorry." Her silence worried him, and he got to his feet, pulling her up with him, and cupped her cheek. "Sameen? Are you okay?"

"No." The word escaped on a harsh whisper, and Peter tensed. At this rate, his fuck ups would soon guarantee she'd never want him as a mate.

"Talk to me." Instead of leading her down to the first floor, he put his back against the railing, his hands on her hips.

"I'm about to meet a bunch of people I can't see who are all counting on me to help find a woman I've never met, and in order to do that, I'll have to talk about how a group of witches kidnapped me, tortured me, *branded* me, and kept me locked away in my own body for so long, I forgot what it was to be free. And the only man—the only *person* I trust in this entire world? Says he knew he was my *mate* before I even learned his name."

The look on her face? Terror. Mixed with frustration.

Peter didn't know how to allay her fears. She was right—about everything. "There's nothing I can say to fix this, sweetheart. You're the only lead we have."

"I'm not a *lead*." After a long moment, Sameen blew out a breath. "Except, I am. Just…don't leave me alone. Please."

"Never." Peter framed her face with his hands—one of them scarred—and he wondered if she could feel the difference. He wanted to kiss her more than he'd wanted anything in his entire life. This woman was strong and brave and even though she'd been through hell, she trusted him. "You are my life, Sameen. I can't explain it. But no one will ever be more important to me than you." He dipped his head, intending to press a chaste kiss to her forehead, but Sameen moved at just the right time and their lips met.

Fireworks exploded behind his shuttered lids, every muscle coming alive as Sameen kissed him back. Her body fit perfectly with his. As if she were made just for him or he for her. When he drew back, her cheeks were flushed and her chest heaved.

"That…" Sameen sagged against him. "Tell me you'll do that again. If we survive this."

"Every day for the rest of our lives if you'll let me." Peter brushed his thumb along her cheek. "I know you're scared, sweetheart. So am I. But my pack and Farren's—or what's left of it—will fight so you never have to be afraid again."

THE GREAT ROOM was easily twice as large as Farren's living room, and someone had lit a fire in the hearth. Liam and Caitlin, Farren and Eli, and Tierney had already claimed various chairs and couches, while Regulus leaned against a pillar in the corner of the room. The myriad of conversations ground to a halt when Peter and Sameen entered, and all eyes focused on her.

"We're going to sit on a couch about fifteen feet in front of us," Peter said as he guided her forward. "Everyone but Livie and Cade are here."

She nodded, and dammit if he couldn't feel her uncertainty. Had the bond already started? The full moon had just passed when he'd met her. This shouldn't be possible. The kiss had left him aching, and he had to sit carefully so Liam wouldn't notice and give him hell for it.

"This is Sameen," he began. "In case anyone doesn't know, she's my mate—if she chooses me someday—and that should mean she's family." Peter met everyone's gazes, in turn, and no one made a move in protest.

At his side, Sameen leaned closer. "What's happening?"

Liam stood, Farren following suit almost immediately. "If our packs haven't learned how to treat a mate we don't know shite about by now," the beta wolf said, "we don't deserve to survive whatever's comin' for us. Not goin' to lie, Peter. Ya' shocked the piss out of us this mornin'. And there isn't one of us here who wouldn't be more comfortable if she wasn't wearing that feckin' brand on her skin. But if ya' say she's yers, then she's yers—even if she doesn't choose to mate with ya'. Any objections?"

Silence filled the space, broken only by the crackling fire in the hearth.

"Good," Farren said and sank back down next to Eli. "Because Mara's been gone for more than forty-eight hours and there's a damn good chance Sameen's the key to findin' her. Can we get to learnin' what she knows?"

Sameen tightened her grip on Peter's hand, and he could feel her fear like it was his own.

"Not yet." Peter met Farren's glare. "She can't see any of you." He went around the room, giving his mate names, whether each person was a werewolf or elemental—or in the case of Eli, some elemental/practitioner hybrid—and what pack they belonged to. "Cade's still in the basement with Livie. She handles security for our pack, and she showed up a few hours ago. We have one more with us, though this isn't his fight. Regulus owns this property. He's a vampire, and he owes me—several of us now—a life debt."

Regulus bowed his head, and at Sameen's confused expression, cleared his throat. "Were you born sightless or is this the result of an injury?"

Twisting her fingers in her lap, Sameen kept her gaze lowered as she answered softly. "The Thirteen would trap me in my own body. They had no use for me unless they'd captured a new elemental. When you can't blink for months or years at a time…I guess this is what happens. Peter gave me some ointment earlier, and I can see light and shadow. Some very muted colors."

"An injury then. May I approach?" Regulus looked to Peter, as if asking his permission as well.

When they'd both nodded, Regulus bent down to stare into Sameen's eyes. "I am going to touch your cheek now, your lower eyelid. Be prepared. My hands are always cold."

From the way she flinched, his hands were likely a hell of a lot more than cold.

"After more than three centuries on this earth, I have learned many things," the vampire said. "Including the types of injuries that can be healed with a few drops of my blood."

Sameen jerked back, turning to Peter and practically launching herself against him.

"He won't turn you, Sameen." Eli's deep voice held understanding. "When we first met him—shite, the day before yesterday—I'd just cocked up a casting so badly, I destroyed part of Farren's house." He stared down at the floor and shook his head. "And the chaos led to the Thirteen taking Mara without any of us knowing."

"That wasn't yer fault," Farren said softly.

Eli pressed a kiss to her cheek. "It was. But that's not the point. Regulus offered me some of his blood to strengthen me so I could try again. It worked. There was a very brief moment of pain, and then everything was just...more."

Sameen blew out a slow breath and angled her head in the vampire's direction. "You think...I could see again?"

"Likely not as you did before. The scarring on your corneas is old and deep. But I do believe I can provide some improvement."

Peter was desperate to be able to look into Sameen's eyes, to see how they changed with her emotions, and to know that she could see the truth in his gaze. That he was falling in love with her after only a day. But there was a small part of him deep inside cowering with fear. What if she saw him as he truly was, scarred and broken, and rejected him?

Get over yourself, asshole. If she can see again, even a little, nothing else matters.

"Peter?" Sameen squeezed his hand. "You trust him?"

"With my life," he answered.

She nodded, though her chest stuttered with her next breath. "Okay."

SAMEEN

Her heart pounded out of control as the dark, shadowy figure knelt in front of her. "A few drops will suffice. You may wish for something to drink afterward to dispel the taste."

"I'll make tea," Caitlin said, and her quick footsteps faded off to Sameen's left.

"We might need somethin' a wee bit stronger." This, from Liam, and he followed his mate.

She'd made a mistake. Why else would they leave the room? She tried to work up the courage to tell the vampire she'd changed her mind, but then Peter wrapped his arm around her waist, and her fears started to ease. At least until Regulus tipped her chin up.

She tensed, a tiny whimper escaping her throat, and several droplets hit her tongue. They were cold, like he was, and tasted so strongly of copper she wanted to throw up, but he released her, and she let Peter's warmth reassure her as she curled against him.

"How long—?" Before she could even finish the sentence, pain consumed her entire being, but it only lasted for a second —not even long enough for her to cry out—then faded into nothing but a memory. Her eyes burned, sending tears tumbling onto her cheeks as she squeezed them shut, and Peter dashed them away.

She didn't want to look. What if nothing had changed?

A light kiss brushed her lips. "Open your eyes, Sameen. Whatever happens, we'll deal with it."

How did he understand her fears so well without her having to say a word? She so very much wanted to see his face. To know what he looked like. To know what *she* looked like.

Cracking her lids slowly, she gasped. The great room was full of color now. Dark wood walls, a forest green and beige rug spread out under the assortment of leather couches.

Everything was still blurry. She couldn't tell the pattern of the rug or see more than the flickering of the flames in the hearth, but she had enough of her sight back to tell the difference between Farren, Eli, and Tierney, who were all sitting across from her.

"Sameen? Did it work?"

Turning to Peter, she took in his face. Black hair, a little unkempt. This close, her vision was sharper, and she reached up and skimmed her fingers along his cheek. His eyes were brown, and the way he was looking at her...

It didn't matter that she had so few memories of her time before the Thirteen imprisoned her. She was certain no one had ever looked at her the way Peter did.

"There's tea," Caitlin said as she and Liam came back into the room. "And whiskey."

Sameen gawked at the height difference between the two. Liam was easily six-foot-four, as big as a prize fighter, and the top of Caitlin's head only came up to his chin.

"Don't be afraid of Liam, sweetheart," Peter said in her ear. "He can be an ass, but Caitlin will put him in his place if need be."

She was more frightened of the vampire staring down at her. "You are something unknown," Regulus said. "Not elemental. Not practitioner. Not fae. Something new."

Did he have to talk about her like she was an object? She'd been nothing for so long that she wanted to be Sameen now. Not "something." But telling him off was definitely not a risk she wanted to take, especially when in the space of a single blink, he crossed the room and leaned against a pillar. She'd never known a being to be able to move that fast.

"Regulus, you owe me a life debt," Peter said as he pressed a cup of tea into Sameen's hands, "which is the only reason I'm going to say this to you. Sometimes, you can be an insensitive asshole."

No one moved. Sameen wasn't even sure if the others in the room were breathing.

"Excuse me?" Regulus asked.

"Something new? Sameen isn't a *thing*. She's a person. And even if there is something *other* about her, she's still, at her core, a human being."

How did Peter know exactly the right thing to say? Exactly how to defend her when she couldn't defend herself? Sameen took a sip of the tea and shifted closer to him as Regulus bowed from across the room.

"My apologies, Sameen. I meant no disrespect."

Farren grabbed the bottle of whiskey and poured a healthy swig into her cup. "All right. We've delayed long enough. Sameen, we need ya' to tell us everythin' ya' know about the Thirteen and what they did to ya.'"

CHAPTER SEVEN

"*I* don't know where to start."

The return of her sight was both reassuring and disorienting. She'd spent so long in the dark, this new world of colors and shapes and the small, distracting movements of those around her made it hard to think. It was overwhelming.

"At the beginnin'?" Farren asked.

Sameen stared down at her fingers, surprised at how long they were. She'd seen Peter's face, but still had no idea what her own looked like. Or even if she wanted to know.

Taking another sip of tea, she let the spiked Earl Grey soothe her tired throat. "I don't remember the beginning. I don't even know how long ago it was. Or what year it is now."

Peter whispered the date in her ear, and tears burned her eyes.

"I think...it's been more than twelve years." How could she have lost so much time? And worse...not known just how long it really was? "I was at university. So I guess...I would have been twenty-two? Twenty-three? I don't even know where. All I remember are the lilies outside my apartment."

———

IF SHE DIDN'T GET a move on, she'd be late for her exam. Sameen slung her bag over her shoulder and pulled the door closed behind her. All day, the headache throbbing behind her eyes had slowed her down. Even the simplest things: making breakfast, showering, getting dressed had taken her longer than they should have.

The intoxicating scent of lilies surrounded her, but there was something wrong about it. Something too sweet. Cloying. She felt like she was walking through quicksand, each step harder and slower than the last. Then...she was face down in the planter of lilies. Why couldn't she get up? Or scream? Everything went silent and dark, but she knew she was moving. First a gentle, swaying motion, then a sharp tug, like she was being shot out of a cannon across the sky. Her stomach lurched, but as nauseous as she was, she couldn't throw up, couldn't open her mouth, couldn't even breathe.

"This is the conduit? You are certain?" A woman's voice broke through the silence, and Sameen opened her eyes. A stone ceiling. She was on her back, cold air flowing over her naked body, and she couldn't move.

"Yes, Celia. There is no doubt." A young woman stepped into her field of vision holding a sharp stone knife, and before Sameen could react, the blade slashed her upper arm. For a few seconds, she felt nothing. But then the cut started to burn like it was on fire. The woman uttered a string of words Sameen couldn't understand, and then light obscured her vision until she squeezed her eyes shut.

"You have done well, Glenna. Ready the iron."

"I PASSED OUT," Sameen said, her voice fading after talking more in the past thirty minutes than she had the entire time she'd been the Thirteen's prisoner. "The next thing I remember is a dark stone cell. I couldn't move. Breathe. Blink. I don't know how they kept me alive that way. No food, no water. I couldn't feel my heart beat. Like...they'd turned me into stone. My eyes were open. By the time they came for me again, it had been so long, my sight was mostly gone."

The sensation of being trapped, of being awake and aware, but unable to move overwhelmed her, and she started to wheeze, the cup tumbling from her grasp.

Peter's warm hand molded to her cheek. "Look at me, Sameen. You're safe. No one's ever going to hurt you again."

His face swam in and out of focus. More out than in, since Regulus had only managed to restore *some* of her sight. The Thirteen had taken so much from her. It didn't matter that Peter's voice held nothing but pure and total conviction. He didn't know the Thirteen like she did.

Next to her, someone moved, and she jerked, squinting at Tierney who was mopping up the mess at her feet.

"I'm so sorry," she choked out with a glance at Regulus. She tried to slide off the couch to help the werewolf, but Peter stopped her with his arm around her waist.

"Relax. It's nothing that can't be fixed."

"He is right," Regulus said mildly. "I have no particular attachment to that rug. If anything, you have done me a favor. There are ten more in the attic that hold more appeal."

Farren held up her hand. "Can we forget about the feckin' rug so someone can explain what the bloody hell a conduit is?"

"I can hold elements. The Thirteen killed dozens of elementals, and Celia—the coven leader—would send some of their power...into me." Sameen shuddered, remembering the pain every time the witch forced her to take in yet another sliver of power her body didn't know what to do with.

Panic flooded her limbs, making her hands tingle and her chest tighten as air rattled around deep inside her, straining to be freed.

"Ye're an elemental?" Liam asked.

"No. I can't *use* the elements. They're just...in me, and that's not natural." How could she explain the utter helplessness of succumbing to a power she had no means to control?

Oh, God. Now that the Thirteen couldn't find her, there was no way she'd ever be able to get all this power *out* of her. Sameen pressed her hand to her stomach. Everything hurt. Her skin. Her bones. Her head. Air, water, and fire started a war inside her, and her muscles locked up, her lids fluttering. Retreating into the quiet darkness of her broken mind, she prayed just this once, she'd escape the pain.

Peter grabbed her and hauled her into his lap. "Sameen? This is what happened when I found you, isn't it? I've got you. I won't let go."

The strength of his embrace steadied her, but she couldn't see his face. That's all she wanted. To focus on his eyes. She tried to say his name, but her lips refused to bend. This was a different kind of hell than being trapped by Celia's magic. This was the pure agony of the fire inside her trying to burn its way free. Of the water straining to wash her away. Of the air determined to scatter her to the four corners of the earth.

"What's wrong with her?" Caitlin rushed over and took a knee next to them.

"It's a seizure." Peter shifted her slightly so he could rub her back. "Damn. She's hot."

"Is this really the time to think with yer dick?" Liam asked.

"I'm not, asshole. She's actually hot. Like a fever."

If only she could talk. She'd tell them Peter was right. At least three times, the Thirteen had kidnapped fire elementals and siphoned off their power. Or...tried to. She had more fire than anything else in her, and the element was *wrong*. It wasn't hers. Wasn't even *whole*. Maybe that's why it kept fighting her. Fighting to be released.

Caitlin whispered a few words with such a sweet accent, they sounded like a song. The air stirred all around Sameen, cooling her cheeks and bringing blessed relief to the overwhelming heat.

Cool fingers draped over her forehead, and another presence stood behind the air elemental. She couldn't see who it was, but she caught the scent of moss and freshly tilled soil, and she knew. Eli.

He whispered something to Caitlin she couldn't hear, then rested his hand over Sameen's heart. The power that flowed into her from his touch was almost as strong as the fire, water, and air that wanted to tear her apart.

Or...stronger.

Relief loosened her frozen muscles, let her breathe easier, and she blinked up at Peter, finding his gaze locked on her as he continued to rub her back.

"What...did you do?" she whispered when Eli rose and backed away with Caitlin at his side.

"I'm not sure." His huff might have been a laugh. "For all we don't know about you, Sameen, there's just as much if not more you don't know about the rest of us."

"We have a book. A practitioner's book," Caitlin said. "When the Thirteen originally broke off from the Inverness Coven, they weren't completely evil. Some of them wanted to use the Spirit element for good. But before long, they realized they were outnumbered, and four of them attempted to leave. Two were killed, and two others escaped. For a time, at least. One of those practitioners was Eli's father, and another was a woman named Diedre. She gave us a book with sigils and drawings that she said would help us fight the Thirteen and protect Mara."

Tierney snorted. "She didn't bother to tell us we'd need Eli to read the feckin' thing."

"Read?" Eli asked. "I didn't read anything. The book..." He unbuttoned his shirt, and Sameen squinted at his chest. She couldn't understand what she was seeing.

"Are those...tattoos?"

"No. When I touched the book—certain pages of it at least—I absorbed the magic and the symbols just...appeared on my skin. I still don't know how. Bloody painful. But it's what let me cast the protection spell that's hiding you from the Thirteen, and just now, one of the symbols started to come alive."

Symbols coming alive? Magic from a former member of the Thirteen helping *ease* her pain? It was all too much. Sameen fumbled for Peter's hand, needing something real to hold onto. Peter was real.

"You don't know what you did to her?" Peter asked.

"No. Not entirely, mate. Whatever magic the book gave me, sometimes, it knows what to do. But Sameen? You don't just have three elements trapped inside you. I sensed Air, Fire, and Water. But multiple fragments of each one. Like echoes."

She didn't want to remember. Her own screams filled her head, and she squeezed Peter's hand even tighter. "Every few months," she began, "they'd come for me. At first, I fought them. There was this brief moment...maybe a minute...where I'd be free from their control after they dropped the spell that held me prisoner in my own body. But they had apprentices—or other prisoners, I never knew—who'd overpower me until they could order me to obey. Eventually, they just chained me to the wall."

Her voice was starting to weaken, and Caitlin offered her a fresh cup of tea.

"When they'd come, they'd bring me to their ritual space—where they branded me—and tie me down on an altar next to an elemental. Fire, Air, and Water. Never Earth. I don't know why. It took three of them to work the spell. It cleaved a person's element into pieces, and they'd send those pieces into me."

A violent shudder ran through her, and she set the tea down before she spilled yet another cup.

"It always felt so...*wrong*. And I don't think it worked like Celia wanted it to. I lost consciousness every time, and I'd come to with the whole coven throwing spell after spell at me."

"Why?" Peter asked as he pressed his thigh to hers. The panic and fear ebbed. Not completely, but enough for her to draw an easy breath.

"Punishment, I think. Or maybe they were trying to activate the element they'd just put into me? They never explained. But it felt like they were tearing me apart."

"Fuckin' bastards," Liam spat. "We're goin' to end them. We just need to find Mara first. Is there anythin' else ya' can tell us about where they had ya' or where they might have taken Mara? Were ya' at the compound we destroyed the whole time?"

"I don't know. I'm sorry. I wish I did." Tears burned her eyes, and she hunched her shoulders as she wiped them away. She'd give anything to be able to help. Both because they'd protected her and because Sameen thought they were the only ones who might be powerful enough to put an end to the Thirteen forever.

Her brand started to ache, then burn, and she stifled a whimper and pressed her fingers to her side.

Across the room, Farren sucked in a sharp breath. "Sameen? What are ya' feelin' right now?"

"The brand. It hurts. But it's not like before. They aren't calling for me or trying to control me. It's like...I'm feeling what they're doing to someone else."

"Liam?" Farren turned to the beta wolf. "Do ya' feel it too?"

"Aye. Just an itch."

Sameen didn't understand what was going on. Why would Liam feel the pain from her brand? Or Farren?

The female alpha snorted. "I think all the marks are

connected. Ever since Fergus tried to carve me up, I've felt the feckin' thing burn now and again. Never understood why."

Eli sprang up, motioning to Caitlin and Tierney to follow him. "There's a page in the book with the control mark all over it. I never understood what the other symbols on the page meant until now. I think…we might be able to use Sameen—her mark—to trace the magic back to its source."

"Fuck me," Liam said. "Ya' three go figure it out. I'm goin' down to the basement and tell Cade to pull his head out of his arse and get back to bein' an alpha. This might be our best chance to find Mara."

CHAPTER EIGHT

The group in the main room scattered, leaving only Peter and Regulus behind. Sameen was exhausted and could barely manage to sit up. At least Peter didn't seem to mind her snuggling against his side.

"Do you want to lie down?" he asked. "Or...are you hungry?"

"She is ravenous. I do not eat food and even I can see that." The vampire huffed as if he could not believe Peter would ever be so stupid. "I know the young one bought enough food to feed the entire countryside. Get her something."

"Will you be okay?" Peter asked.

He was only going to the kitchen. Not that she knew where the kitchen was in this house, but it couldn't be far. Still, she'd been near hysterics earlier at the thought he might leave her alone.

Her throat was raw from all the talking, and she couldn't stomach any more tea, so she just nodded, and he rushed off.

Only then did she realize she was now alone with a vampire. This was a mistake. She had to go find Peter.

"I will not harm you," Regulus said as if he were discussing the weather. "And before you ask, those as old as I am have many *talents*. If I desired, I could see all of your thoughts. Even force you to bend to my will."

Sameen tried to get up, but the room started to spin. Regulus was at her side before she even realized what was happening and caught her elbow.

"I am not a bastard, Sameen. I am, as Peter said, an insensitive asshole. But that comes from centuries without my humanity. When I gave you my blood, it created a connection between us. That connection will fade in another few hours. But for now, I can sense your pain. Physical and emotional." He eased her back down to the leather sofa. His voice was familiar, and stirred a memory buried deep in the back of her mind. Cursing. His.

"You were their prisoner too."

"For a time. Eli's father freed me at great risk to his own life." Regulus leaned closer and rested his fingers at her temple.

Bars. A cell. Ribbons of bright metal all through the stone floor shimmered in the candlelight. Chains rattled, and then footsteps.

"I will not survive another bloodletting," Regulus managed, his voice a shadow of its current deep baritone. "Unless they wish to hasten the end of my existence."

A man dressed in a black cloak with a hood shadowing his face withdrew a set of keys from his pocket and unlocked the cell door. He didn't speak as he approached. Paulo was the Thirteen's slave, bound years before, though in the weeks Regulus had been locked in this cell, the man had been...almost kind.

"Stake me. Please. Starvation and blood loss is an agonizing end."

The man knelt next to Regulus and pulled back the hood. His eyes held such pain as he exposed his neck.

"Why?" Regulus asked.

Paulo shook his head, pointed to his neck, and leaned closer.

With a snarl, the vampire yanked the man against him, his bound hands trembling as he sank his fangs deep. Blood rushed into his mouth, and it tasted better than any he'd had in his very long existence.

Strength flooded his limbs in stark contrast to the weakening man in his grasp.

Paulo hissed out a breath and pressed his hand to his side. Regulus withdrew his fangs from the human's neck, then pricked his own finger and touched the blood to each of the wounds he'd left behind.

"They are calling to you."

A nod from Paulo, and another grimace of pain.

"Do you have the keys to these shackles?" the vampire asked. At the shake of the man's head, Regulus sighed. "Then I will have to do this the old fashioned way. It will be loud. And painful."

Paulo glanced back at the corridor, then met Regulus's gaze and gestured with his hands. Left, straight, left again, up, then right. His face twisted in pain, and he scrambled to his feet, swaying slightly.

"I could take you with me," Regulus offered.

Paulo shook his head and darted a glance outside the cell. Motioning for the vampire to hurry, he rushed off in the opposite direction he'd told Regulus to go.

Staring down at the silver manacles around his wrists, Regulus grit his teeth and closed his eyes. The pain pulled a groan from his throat, and the silver links snapped, freeing his arms.

He could feel Paulo's suffering. Having the man's blood—almost enough to drain him completely—gave Regulus a window into the human's soul. He hated himself, hated what he'd become, but most of all, he feared he'd not done enough to protect his son.

If Regulus had any chance of defeating the Thirteen, he'd stay. Fight. Try to save the man who'd saved him. But though vampires were one of the strongest creatures to walk this earth, he was powerless against magic.

There was no more time. He had to run. Now.

"What the fuck are you doing?" Peter growled.

Regulus was across the room before Sameen could blink. "Sharing a memory. That is all."

"Don't touch her. No one touches her." Her werewolf held something in his hands she couldn't quite make out until he stalked over to her and set a steaming bowl down on the table. "Are you all right?" he asked Sameen, linking their fingers.

"Fine. And you're not my keeper. Regulus wasn't hurting me." She jerked her hands from his and reached for the bowl. Soup. Chicken soup. Oh, God. How long had it been since she'd eaten a hot meal?

After the first spoonful, some of her anger faded. "Thank you for this."

The vampire cleared his throat. "I must check on the young one. Peter, the life debt I owe you extends to your mate as well. I will not—cannot—harm either of you for as long as I walk this plane." He streaked halfway across the room, stopped, and turned back to them. "I fear for you, my friend. Your temper has worsened every day I have known you. If you do not learn to control it, you will lose...everything."

PETER

After Sameen finished the soup, she curled against him and was asleep in minutes. Regulus's words played on a loop in Peter's head. He knew he hadn't been the easiest person to get along with since the fire in Bellingham. But could anyone blame him? He had a permanent limp, and for fuck's sake, couldn't even manage to carry his *mate* back to the mansion when he'd found her. He'd had to call Liam to do it for him.

A door opened at the other end of the house, and a moment later, Livie strode into the room. She stopped short when she saw him, and he hadn't realized how much he'd missed the other half of his family.

"She's gorgeous," Livie said softly. "And you look like you're already over the moon for her. What's her story? Liam said she could help us figure out where they have Mara?"

Peter stared down at his mate and ran his hand over her thick black locks. "She was their prisoner, Livie. For a long time. And I don't know if she'll be able to love anyone—trust anyone—after what they did to her."

"You think it was easy for Caitlin to love again? Or even Cade? When it's your mate, you find a way. Even if it takes months. Years." Livie ran a hand through her hair, pushing it back from her cheek to reveal a web of burn scars that weren't all that different from Peter's. They'd both been unable to shift out of their wolf forms after the fire that had allowed Katerina to kidnap Cade and torture him for almost a year. Yet for some reason, Livie wasn't angry. She didn't curse her slower, loping gait or the fact that she couldn't raise her left arm fully. She'd accepted her injuries, her limitations, and never looked back.

Why couldn't he do the same? Peter pressed a gentle kiss to Sameen's head. "I'm going to fuck this up."

"No. You won't." Cade stood behind Livie, his eyes haunted, three days of stubble darkening his jaw. "Because when it's your mate, you find a way."

The urge to stand, to do something for his alpha, like shove Cade down on the couch and feed him a fucking sandwich reared up inside, but the warm, reassuring weight of his mate in his arms stopped him. "Cade."

"Can she really help us find Mara?"

"I don't know." Peter didn't understand most of what Caitlin, Eli, and Tierney did with that book. "She has the Thirteen's mark, and she, Farren, and Liam all felt their marks flare at the same time. Caitlin thinks they're all connected somehow."

Cade paled even further and braced his hands against the

back of the couch Livie sat on. His fingers dug into the leather hard enough Peter heard wood crack under the strength of his grip. "If they've done anything to Mara...*anything—*"

"They'll pay." Peter understood now in a way he never had. How he was willing to die for the woman in his arms, even though he knew nothing about her. Even though he had no idea if she wanted him. If she'd ever want him.

"What's her name?" Cade was still leaning heavily on the couch, and Livie cast a quick glance back at him, worry tightening her lips.

"Sameen."

"Bossman? You need to eat something before you fall over." Livie arched her brows as she turned back to Peter. "And you? When was the last time *you* ate anything?"

Shit. He didn't have any idea. Yesterday?

"Has *anyone* had a proper meal since getting here?" With a huff, Livie popped up and shook her head. "Men. Useless. All of you. If we're going on the offensive, we're *not* doing it on empty stomachs. Now where's the kitchen?"

Peter pointed, and Livie turned on a heel and headed down the hall, leaving him alone with his alpha. What the hell did he say to the man? He'd been an ass for months. And Cade looked like he was about to fall over. "You know we won't stop until we get her back, right?"

Cade sank down onto the couch and dropped his head into his hands. "I love this pack. Never wanted to be alpha. But after Mike died, it fit. *I* fit. Without Mara...I can't keep doing this. Hell, I don't know how to live without her."

Before Peter could shift Sameen out of his arms so he could take a seat next to his alpha and try to comfort him, try to find *something* to say that would make any of this even slightly better, Cade jerked up. "I need a shower." He stopped only a few inches from Peter and stared down at him. "Don't fuck up with her, man. If you do, you'll regret it for the rest of your life."

CHAPTER NINE

MARA

"**W**ake up!"

She tried to force her eyes open, but every cell in her body wanted to stay asleep. What did it matter anyway? She'd be dead soon.

Why wasn't she upset about that?

"Because those damn practitioners are messing with you. Wake up! Now!"

Mara cracked her lids, but she couldn't see anything beyond the faint outline of the cell bars in front of her. She lay on the thin mattress, cradling her rapidly growing belly.

"Better. You have to fight."

"Can't," she whispered. She had to obey. Had to listen to Celia. Sleep when the lights were off. Wake when they were on. Eat all the food she was given. Let them take her baby. Accept her fate.

"No. We're going to stop them."

How? Mara was locked in a cell, the Thirteen's sigil burned

81

into her side, and she was—by her estimation—at least six months pregnant now. Werewolf babies were born at seven months. Three or four more days and she'd give birth to a daughter she'd never know. All so a crazed group of practitioners could use her baby to channel this mythical element she wasn't even sure existed.

"It exists."

"You couldn't have shared this information with me earlier?" Mara whispered. "Or maybe warned me when you were going to take over my body? I don't even know who you are—what you are."

"I'm you. And a little bit of Katerina."

Great. So she had multiple personalities inside her. This wasn't getting any better. Or giving her any hope. She couldn't fight the Thirteen's magic. Even now, all she wanted to do was sleep.

"You can fight. But you have to want it."

Did she? She loved Cade. Loved their baby. Rachel Eleanor Bowman. Her daughter had a name. She wasn't some vessel to be *used* and manipulated by power-hungry lunatics.

As if the baby knew what Mara needed, she kicked—hard.

Mara pulled the blanket up to her chin and felt for the brand under the thin gown they'd given her. No. The gray dress they'd *forced* her to put on. Celia hadn't *given* her anything. Her wrists ached from when they'd tied her down. This wasn't how she wanted to die. Alone. Afraid. Without her mate. Without ever knowing their daughter.

"I want it."

"Good."

***

MARA DIDN'T KNOW how much time passed before the lights came back on, but she'd managed to stay awake since her sister

—or whatever part of her sister had locked on to her own fire element—had started yelling at her.

As she pushed up to sitting, the cramp took her by surprise, and she hissed in pain. A contraction. Not labor. Not yet. But the baby was definitely running out of time. And Mara was too.

She expected one of the witches or their apprentices to come with a tray of food for her based on the empty, gnawing sensation in her stomach, but instead, the younger practitioner, Freya, stalked down the corridor with two of the black-robed servants in her wake. "Get up, elemental."

Mara struggled to rise, hungry and dizzy, bracing her hand on the wall for support. The very cold, magic-infused wall. She could feel it seeping into her skin, and jerked her fingers back when Freya made the center portion of the bars disappear.

"Bind her."

"Why?" Mara asked. "You know I can't fight you."

Freya sneered at her prisoner. "Because I want them to."

The two men, their hoods drawn low, each took one of Mara's arms, pinned them behind her, and tied her wrists tightly. Mara whimpered when they fastened a blindfold over her eyes until Freya told her to shut up.

"Pay attention," the fire elemental hissed silently. *"Steps. Turns."*

Mara tried, but she was so hungry, she wasn't sure she'd counted correctly. A flight of stairs left her winded, and she almost collapsed at the top. Only the firm grip the two minions had on her arms kept her upright.

But then she smelled it. Fresh air. Wherever she was...there was an open door or window close by. *Cade. Please find me. I'm scared. I need you.*

"Place her on the altar," Freya ordered.

Oh God. Not again.

They worked quickly, securing her wrists over her head, binding her ankles tightly together, and tying them to the stone.

All Mara wanted to do was ask what was going on, but she couldn't seem to form the words. Without her sight, all she could do was listen. Multiple sets of footsteps. Not just Freya. And she could smell Celia. The witch wore a perfume or lotion that smelled like something rotten—or maybe it was just the woman's magic.

"She is ready," Freya said. The practitioner's voice grated, and the fire elemental railed against Mara's inability to speak.

"The babe will serve our purposes well, but we must know how strong she is." Celia's words chilled her to her core. "This will hurt, elemental."

Mara moaned and tried to form words, and Freya laughed. "I told her to shut up."

"Childish, sister. Even if I do not wish to hear her pleas and whines, I enjoy hearing her submit to me." Leaning closer so her breath ghosted across Mara's cheek, Celia whispered, "You may speak, elemental. For now."

"What are you doing?" Mara asked. "Everything hurts, and I'm worried about the baby." The urge to call Rachel *her* baby was overwhelming, but she had to convince Celia she'd accepted her fate.

"We are testing to see how well the babe can absorb the elements we've taken over the years. And if the casting is successful, you will bring us everything we need before you die."

"Before I die...?" Did Celia mean now? "I thought...you needed the baby to be born?" Tears burned Mara's eyes behind the blindfold. She needed more time. Time with Rachel, even if she couldn't hold her daughter like she wanted to. Time to figure out how she and the fragments of her sister's element could resist Celia's magic. Time for Cade to find her.

"Oh, we do, elemental. I have seen her birth. The three Fates have shown me much in my lifetime, and I believe the baby is our destiny. But we would be foolish not to test the child before the end. When we perform the final ritual, we will only have one chance to form the Spirit element. And we must locate our missing conduit."

"Conduit?"

"Another being. For many years, we thought she was the answer. But she was never strong enough to absorb the four elements. Earth, in particular, resisted. Every time. She escaped when your mate and the rest of those fucking mongrels attacked our summer home, and they are protecting her. But we will *retrieve* her."

"Just please...don't hurt the pack. My mate. Do whatever you want to me," Mara sobbed, "just leave them alone."

"Gag her," Celia ordered. "I am weary of her pleas, but I will enjoy her screams. If this works, there will not be much left of her mind, and that will be a blessing."

Mara didn't fight when they shoved a thick piece of leather between her teeth and fastened it behind her head. Whatever they were planning...it was going to hurt.

"I'm taking over," Katerina—or at least the shred of Katerina left by the fire agate crystal embedded in Mara's chest—said.

Within the space of a single breath, Mara was trapped in the small, inescapable box she always found herself in when the fire took over.

"Why?" she asked the fire.

"Because at the end of this, you need to be the one who lives. I tried to take everything from you once. I will not do it again."

Several practitioners started to chant, and the altar rumbled underneath her body. A frigid wind whipped through the ritual space, and Celia shouted, "Air!"

It didn't matter that Katerina tried to protect her, the pain of having an abundance of an element not her own forced into her body—into her baby's body—made her feel like she was being ripped apart from the inside out. Rachel kicked, her little arms and legs flailing, and warmth filled Mara's belly. Almost as if her daughter were channeling the fire to protect herself.

"Are you there?" Mara asked the other part of her fractured mind. *"Say something."*

All she heard were her own screams.

"Water!" Celia's shout reverberated against the stone walls, and the sudden influx of humidity made it hard to breathe. Mara tried to suck in as much of her own element as she could from the deep, dark place she'd been forced into, and it strengthened her slightly. But not enough. She pulled at the restraints, desperate, and the skin of her wrists burned and tore. The baby calmed slightly to Mara's relief, but her mind started to crack, so overwhelmed by the multiple elements inside her. The part that was Mara stayed hidden safely away, but her other half? Katerina? Whatever this *presence* was?

Mara could feel it slipping away.

When Celia called for fire, Mara heard one conscious thought in her sister's voice.

"The sigil has magic of its own. Use it."

The entire room started to shake, and the *thunks* and *chinks* of small bits of rocks hitting the floor terrified her. She couldn't take any more. Neither could the fire element inside her. Or her baby. The Thirteen would kill her and Rachel if they didn't stop.

Celia and the others were still chanting, until in unison they shouted, "Earth!"

Even the protection of being locked in the deep recesses of her own mind couldn't spare Mara from the pure agony of the Earth element being channeled into her body. Earth was stability. Grounding. A foundation. It didn't take to being manipulated.

Her wails started to fade. She was too weak to even cry out anymore. Her back arched as every muscle in her body seized. But the power? It flowed through her like nothing she'd ever experienced before. The baby felt it too, and when Celia called for silence, Mara sensed her daughter's attempts to hold on to the energy and find a way to send it back to those hurting her mother.

Hands pressed to her belly, and Celia cackled with glee. "This child will bring us Spirit. She is strong, and once we brand her with our mark, she will be ours for all eternity."

"No! They can't touch her! Do something!" Mara pled with her other half to fight, to even respond to her, but there was only silence.

The ropes around her wrists and ankles fell away, and Freya ordered her to stand. Mara's body didn't move, and someone slapped her cheek, hard. "Stand up, bitch."

Rough fingers ripped the blindfold away. Mara's eyes were open, the old stone ceiling directly above her head now with fresh scorch marks from whatever the Thirteen had done to call for fire.

"I told you," Celia said sharply. "Sending all four elements into her would not leave much of her mind intact. Take her back to her cell and turn off the lights. Once she sleeps for a time, there might be enough of her consciousness left for her to eat. Otherwise, we will have to force feed her."

As the black-robed men grabbed her and headed out of the ritual space, Freya asked, "What about the conduit and the elemental's mate?"

"Once we have the child, they will be the first ones to die. You will have your revenge. Glenna's death will not be in vain. You may even play with the wolf for as long as you wish before you end him. Make him suffer."

No! Not Cade!

Mara needed to get the hell out of this mental trap her sister had forced her into and try to warn Cade. Katerina had told her to use the magic in the sigil. But how? Dammit. Why hadn't her sister told her this before? When she could have asked questions.

Celia's lackeys all but dropped her onto the mattress,

mumbled a few words to close the bars, and walked away. The lights flickered out, but though Mara couldn't move, she wasn't asleep either.

She could sense her sister's element, but it wasn't as strong as it had been. It was broken. Dying.

Focusing on Cade and on the life growing inside of her, Mara let out a silent scream. The pain overwhelmed her, and she almost passed out before she found the strength to move. The other part of her had taken on this pain, sacrificed so Mara could survive. And now...Katerina's consciousness—if it was even still alive—retreated so Mara could take control once again.

"I won't give up," she whispered. "I'll get us out of here."

She was so weak, it took her several long moments before she could move her arm enough to place her hand over the sigil burned into her skin. When she did, though, it flared against her palm. Heat pulsed, like it was calling to her fire. To Rachel's fire.

If she used her element, the practitioners would know, and they'd make her suffer. Her body couldn't take another assault, and she couldn't do that to her baby.

"Cade...please. Hear me. I'm alive. You have to find me."

Her heart skipped a beat, and then the most intense longing and need she'd ever felt consumed her, giving her strength where moments ago, she'd had none.

He was alive. And he'd heard her. Cade would never stop looking for her. She just hoped he'd be in time.

CHAPTER TEN

CADE

$\mathcal{E}$verything he did reminded him of Mara. The four-poster bed in the lavish bedroom had an emerald green duvet that matched her eyes. Someone had packed a suitcase for them at Farren's, and when Cade opened it, her scent surrounded him. His hair was still damp from the shower, and he tugged on a Seattle Seahawks sweatshirt. One of the first she'd bought him when her element had freed him from the fire charm trapping him as his wolf.

He fingered the wedding ring hanging from a chain around his neck. Around the full moon, he always took it off and secured it on the chain. Otherwise, it would fall off when he shifted. Now, it felt wrong not to be wearing it. But he had to be ready for anything. For the Thirteen to attack them. Even here. Hell, Ewan could turn on everyone in a heartbeat. Or...lack of one.

Digging out a pair of socks, Cade froze. Whoever had packed had grabbed Mara's journal. She'd started writing in the little, leather-bound book after they'd found out about the baby, but she'd never let Cade read any of it.

Cade opened the journal and flipped to the last page.

I don't know what to call you. Peanut? Nugget? Little bean? I hope you read this some day, so I don't want to tell you what names we've picked out for you. Because what if we change our minds once we meet you?

I feel you kick and I love you so much already. But I'm scared. Aunt Caitlin thinks once you're born, everything will be okay. But I'm not so sure. What if the fire making me sick hurts you too? I have this terrible feeling something bad is going to happen and I won't be able to stop it.

I'm supposed to protect you. But most of the time I can't even protect myself and I'd never forgive myself if something happened to you.

When I close my eyes, I imagine what you'll be like when you're born. Will your eyes be like mine? Or like your daddy's? Will you have his smile? His strength?

I laugh thinking about your fiery curls when you burn a hole in the carpet the first time I make you clean your room, and I can't even begin to tell you how proud I'll be of you the first time you shift.

The world we're bringing you into is so complicated, and there's nothing I wouldn't give to shield you from it. At least for a little while. I hope all my fears turn out to be silly. But if they aren't, know that your daddy and I love you.

Cade slammed the book shut, tears burning his eyes. He had to get his mate back. Had to make sure she and their pup were safe. If he failed, he wasn't sure he could go on.

Taking the stairs two at a time, he ran right into Sameen and Peter on his way to a large rec room Caitlin, Eli, and Tierney had appropriated for their work on Diedre's book. Peter's poor mate yelped and started to go down, her socks slipping on the polished tile floors, and Cade instinctively grabbed her around the waist.

The second his hand touched her side, she cried out, and an intense burst of heat flared under his palm.

"Cade...please. Hear me. I'm alive. You have to find me."

"Mara," Cade growled just as Peter got in his face.

"Let. Go. Of. Her," the younger wolf snapped, and if Cade hadn't been so completely focused on his mate's voice in his head, he probably would have punched Peter for daring to speak to him that way.

Instead, he kept one hand pressed to her side and shifted the other under her elbow. "No," he said sharply. "She's connecting me to Mara. Somehow."

"What?" Peter froze, his gaze locked on Sameen's. "Can you do that?"

"I...I don't know." Her voice trembled, and the fear written all over her face? Cade couldn't keep hold of her for long.

"Give me just a few seconds. Please." He closed his eyes and focused on the intense love he and Mara shared, how desperate he was to find her, and his promise to never stop looking for her. It was all he had. All he could think to tell her, but maybe it would be enough.

As quickly as it had flared up, the connection, the magic flowing from Sameen into him, faded away, and Cade stepped back, holding his hands up in case Peter decided to be an ass.

Who was he kidding? Peter was always an ass.

But the other wolf didn't attack, didn't even spare Cade a second look. He just gathered Sameen in his arms and smoothed a hand over her hair. "Are you all right?"

"I think so. I've never felt the mark do...*that.*"

At her words, Cade understood. "That was the Thirteen's brand? Where I touched you?"

She nodded and pulled up her t-shirt. The burned skin glowed, the light pulsing once before dying out, and Cade looked to Peter, then Sameen. "Can I try again? Only if you agree."

Caitlin came up behind the not-yet-mated pair. "What's goin' on?"

"My mark...it let Cade feel Mara," Sameen whispered, then squinted up at the alpha wolf. "It hurt. But go ahead."

A growl rumbled in Peter's chest, and Sameen leaned back against him while Cade touched her side as gently as he could. Nothing. No spark. No warmth beyond that of her skin, and no sign of his mate.

"I'm sorry," she said as Cade dropped his hand. "I wish—"

"Don't." Fuck. He'd been a terrible alpha ever since she'd been taken. "You don't apologize. If anything, I need to ask you to forgive me. I should never have touched you for a second longer than it took to stop you from falling. Peter's claimed you, and even if he hadn't, no other male in the world gets to put his hands on you unless you agree to it."

Sameen clung to Peter, peering up at Cade with watery, pale brown eyes. "You're the alpha? Peter's alpha?"

Shit. How could he have forgotten the woman could barely see? That she'd never met him? Liam had recounted a bit of what she'd been through: kept in chains, blinded, unable to move for months or even years, and he'd just put his hands all over her.

Shame raised a lump in his throat. "Yeah."

"Don't mind him, luv," Farren said, joining Caitlin. "He's been an arse for three days now. Bein' away from his mate while she's carryin' their pup? He's got a bloody good reason, but that's no excuse."

The rebuke from the female alpha stung, but she wasn't wrong. When they got Mara back—if they got Mara back—he was going to spend every day for the rest of his life making up for all of his failings. To Mara. To his pack. To Farren.

"Can we...can I sit down?" Sameen asked. "I'm a little dizzy."

Peter didn't hesitate to wrap an arm around her waist and lead her into the next room. Farren elbowed Cade in the ribs.

"Get on in there with them. And try to be a mite less growly, will ya'? Livie and I are goin' to bring a mess of food in for everyone."

"Farren?" Cade didn't move, his feet seemingly rooted to the spot as he watched the only connection he had to his mate shuffle away in Peter's embrace. "You understand, don't you?"

"That I do. But that wee girl has been through some shite. We all have at the hands of those magical bastards, but what happened to her? I know ya' lost yerself when ya' were trapped as yer wolf. But ya' had thirty-some odd years before that to figure out who ya' were, and a mate who knew exactly how to bring ya' back. That one? They stripped her of everythin'. Locked her in her own body—awake and aware but unable to move, scream, or even blink her fuckin' eyes. So before ya' say a word in there, remember that. None of us will stop until we find Mara and every member of the Thirteen is dead. I give ya' my word."

There was so much Cade wanted to say to Farren, but she spun on her heel and strode away, leaving him yearning for his mate and afraid even if he did find her, he'd lose his pack in the process.

<hr>

SAMEEN

Cade, though not as tall or as broad as Liam, had a presence about him Sameen didn't need perfect vision to see. It was in the man's energy. His very being.

Peter had almost lost control when Cade had put his hands on her, but he'd backed down at his alpha's tone. At least in part. Sameen had felt his outrage and his total and complete commitment to protecting her somehow as he'd held her. Like they were already connected.

She knew so little about werewolves. The Thirteen had talked about them from time to time, along with vampires and fae, but she couldn't remember having any actual contact with them. Not before she was taken.

And now she was apparently part of a family of them. A family gathered in yet another room in this huge house... waiting for her.

The walls were all muted colors and dark wood. A big screen at the other end of the room glowed, but she couldn't read what was on it from what had to be twenty or thirty feet away. Plush carpet pillowed her feet, and she was grateful she didn't have to worry about slipping like she had in the hallway.

"Sameen? Over here," Caitlin called from a grouping of chairs next to a large window.

Outside, darkness held sway, and she stifled a shudder. For the rest of her life, she never wanted to be anywhere dark and cold again. Peter still held her, but Sameen took her own chair, tucking her legs under her and hugging herself tightly. Peter dropped into the seat next to her, and though they weren't touching any longer, she could still feel him. His possessiveness. His worry. His frustration.

"What just happened out there?" Caitlin asked.

"I don't know." Sameen rubbed her side and winced. The brand *hurt*. "Whenever the Thirteen marked someone with the sigil, I knew. Like we were all linked together, suffering as one. I could never cry for any of them—Celia's spell prevented it—but in some awful, terrible way, knowing there were others out there in the Thirteen's control? It made me feel like I wasn't so very alone."

Caitlin reached out and squeezed Sameen's hand. "When I was sixteen, a boy I thought I might have loved bound my air to his earth. His name was Fergus Tharp, and the Thirteen branded him like they branded you. At least half a dozen elementals died when he...forced me to help him take their powers. We failed. Every time."

The pain in Caitln's voice made Sameen's heart hurt, and she gripped the woman's fingers tightly. "For how long? Was he one of the ones I...could feel?"

"He died a few months ago. If you were their prisoner for twelve years...they branded him before they took you. But...yes. He was one of the ones you could feel."

Cade cleared his throat. "Are you telling me those fuckers branded Mara?"

Sameen didn't want to answer him, but something about his presence didn't give her much choice. "I'm sorry. But yes. When you touched me..."

"I'm going to kill them," he swore.

"Cade? That was always the plan," Liam said, clapping a hand on his alpha's shoulder. "They've tried to end every one of us, and anyone who hurts Mara...ya' know how we all feel about her."

Caitlin picked up a large book, turning it so Sameen could peer down at the pages. "I don't know how much of this ya' can read...?"

"Everything's blurry." Sameen held out her hand. As soon as Caitlin gave her the book, its power sent a shudder through her. "I can feel it, though."

Eli reached over her shoulder, and the movement had her gasping, sending the book tumbling to the floor.

"Watch it, man," Peter growled. "You're scaring her."

"Fuck me. I'm sorry." Eli skirted the chair to retrieve the old tome, flipped through the pages, and offered it to Sameen again. "I didn't think."

"N-no. It's not your fault. I'm just...not used to this. People."

It was more than that. So much of her current existence was baffling to her. Being able to move, to see, to speak. It had been so long and she was so very broken. Every part of her.

From the chair next to her, a low rumble in Peter's chest started to grow louder, and the sound was so possessive it was almost soothing.

"Relax, mate. You know I've only eyes for Farren," Eli said and dropped to a knee next to Sameen's chair. "This page is the one I think we need. Do you need me to describe it to you?"

With a shake of her head, Sameen lifted the book closer and squinted. "The control sigil is in the center?"

"Yes."

In a ring around the mark she'd wear for the rest of her life were a variety of other symbols. The moon, the Tree of Life, and more she didn't recognize. "I don't know what most of these others are."

"Runes," Caitlin said. "That first one is Ansuz. It represents a signal or message received. With its position, I think it's referrin' to the way the Thirteen use the control sigil. They send warnings, knowledge, or simply pain across the link created by the sigil. Opposite Ansuz is Nauthiz." The air elemental shuddered and rubbed her upper arms. "It's the rune of constraint and pain. Here, it's reversed, which tells me Ansuz—the message—is what's bringin' the pain."

Sameen wasn't sure she could take much more of this. Every symbol Caitlin pointed out gave her less hope she'd ever be free from the Thirteen's control. Not knowing what to do or say, she reached for Peter's hand.

When his warm fingers gripped hers, the calm, reassuring presence she desperately needed—the one she'd yearned for the entire time she'd been a prisoner—soothed her. Was this man really her mate? Why else would she react to him so strongly? Why else would she need him like she needed food and water and sunlight?

"Go on," she said. As long as Peter kept hold of her hand, she'd be okay. At least...she hoped she would be.

"The last rune is Isa. It's between Ansuz and Nauthiz and

represents stasis. When Isa rules, nothin' can change. Ye're trapped by the signals the Thirteen are sendin', and that's what causes ya' such pain."

"Is this supposed to make me feel better?" Sameen asked. "Or help us find Mara?"

"Yes and no." Caitlin looked to Eli, and the practitioner turned the page.

"That same grouping of runes around the control sigil are repeated here. Multiple times. I think this might represent all the different times the Thirteen branded someone."

"How do ya' know that?" Liam asked.

Eli stepped between Sameen and Cade. "Because last week, there were six separate groupings on this page. Now...there are seven."

CHAPTER ELEVEN

PETER

Cade practically vibrated with anger. Not that Peter could blame him. To see evidence of your mate's suffering in black and white? Or...black and the aged yellowish hue the old pages had taken on over the years?

Liam stood next to the alpha wolf, clearly ready to restrain the man in a heartbeat.

"Will ya' get to the bloody point?" Farren asked. "How does any of this help us find Mara?"

Eli rolled up his sleeve. "When I touched that first page a couple of hours ago, this showed up on my arm."

Everyone—except for Sameen, who was too far away to see exactly what Eli was showing them—tensed, and Farren swore loudly. "Fuck. And ya' didn't think to tell me? That's the Thirteen's sigil, Eli. How the hell are ya' supposed to keep us all safe if they're controllin' ya?" She practically threw herself at her mate, wrapping her arms around him and holding on so tightly, Eli grunted.

"Can't...breathe, love."

"I don't much care. Rather you unconscious than under their control."

Peter had never seen the female alpha display quite so much emotion, and he reached over the took Sameen's hand again, needing this new, very tenuous mate bond to keep him grounded.

"Farren, calm down," Caitlin said. "Look at the sigil. Really look."

Eli extricated himself and held out his arm so his mate could see the new mark clearly. Peter leaned forward. "That's different from what's in the book."

"It is." Caitlin went on to explain that the inked version of the sigil on Eli's forearm had an unbroken circle around it, which she believed meant the Thirteen couldn't sense it or channel their magic through it in any way. "I think Eli can send some of *his* power through this mark to Sameen's. If she's outside the wards that protect this place and Eli momentarily drops the casting keeping the Thirteen from sensing her...it could work. Her mark could activate all the others. If he combines his magic with an air location charm, maybe...?"

"It could lead us to Mara," Cade finished. "Do it."

"Hold on a minute." Peter released Sameen's hand, pushed to his feet, and stalked over to his alpha. "We're talking about causing Sameen a hell of a lot of pain. And putting her at risk of the Thirteen finding her. This isn't a decision *you* get to make on your own."

"I want to help." Her voice was so quiet, Peter almost didn't hear her over the roar of his own heartbeat in his ears. "I'll do it."

"Sameen..."

Tears glistened in her eyes. "I've shared the pain of every single person to ever wear this mark. When Mara reached out earlier? She must be very strong, because I didn't only hear her words. I felt what she felt. It was..." Sameen shook her head. "She's terrified. She needs to know she's not alone."

Peter grabbed her hands and pulled her to her feet. "Can we talk about this? Privately? Please?"

"You won't change my mind."

Peter's heart cracked, and the gaping wound throbbed with every breath. "I can't lose you."

"Until yesterday, you didn't have me." She sniffled, staring down at the floor. "I didn't have a life before I escaped. Not one I remember, anyway. I couldn't speak, couldn't see, couldn't even move of my own free will, and now? I'm warm, clothed, and surrounded by people who don't know me at all, but have protected me. No one more than you."

With a heavy sigh, she reached up to lay her hand against Peter's cheek. "You make me feel like a person."

"You *are* a person. A very special one. My mate. Even if you don't accept me. Even if once the Thirteen are dead, you leave and I never see you again, you will always be the most important person in my life. I would die to keep you safe, don't you understand that?" His anger simmered just under his skin, and his wolf asserted himself with a feral growl. He ached to throw Sameen over his shoulder and carry her upstairs, away from Eli, Caitlin, Cade...anyone who thought using her and activating her sigil was anything but a terrible, horrible idea.

"What I understand," she said, her voice taking on an edge he hadn't heard before, "is that you want to control what I do. The Thirteen took every one of my choices away for more than twelve years. I'll be damned if I'm going to let you do the same."

Shock stayed his steps as Sameen pushed past him and headed for the door, only pausing once she'd crossed the threshold.

"I need a few minutes. A bathroom. And shoes, if we're leaving the house. Can someone help me...?" she asked.

"Let me," Caitlin said and rushed after her. "Do you want to take my arm?"

The two women left the room, Sameen's hand tucked in the crook of Caitlin's elbow, and Caitlin whispering quietly to her.

Peter balled his hands into fists and let out a low, frustrated growl. Until Cade grabbed him by the shoulders and shoved him up against the nearest wall. "Look, asshole. I know I've been a shit alpha the past few days. Hell, ever since Mara started losing time. But if you don't get yourself under control, you're going to lose her before you ever have a chance to find out if she cares about you."

"Get off of me." Peter tried to jab Cade in the stomach, but his left arm failed him, sending pain radiating down his side, and he sucked in a sharp breath. "Fuck, that hurts."

"Did you miss the part about me being *your alpha*?" Cade's snarled words forced Peter's wolf to back down instinctually, and he slumped in the other man's grip. "That's better. Two choices. You either listen to what I have to say, or you can leave this pack once we find Mara. You know my rules. Know they haven't changed since I took over for Mike years ago. We're a family. And family sticks. You haven't claimed Sameen. The way you're acting, you might never get the chance. But that doesn't matter. She's your mate, so she's family too."

"You're asking her to sacrifice herself. To put herself back in the Thirteen's hands. They'll kill her, Cade. You know they will."

"If you took a minute to pull your head out of your ass," his alpha grumbled.

"We're not going to let the Thirteen take her again," Eli said. "We're going to try this before dawn. Regulus can join us. We'll be six wolves, an elemental, me, and a vampire."

"Two vampires." Everyone whirled around at Regulus's voice to find him and Ewan standing in the doorway. "The young one has completed his transition, and even as his wolf, my *talents* can keep him in line should he lose control. No one who attempts to harm your mate will live to see the sun, Peter. That, I can promise you."

SAMEEN

Caitlin led her upstairs and into a lavishly furnished bedroom. "Ya' look like ya' might be about Farren's size."

"What?" Sameen was too busy trying to get her bearings. This wasn't the room she'd shared with Peter. It didn't smell the same. But she had no idea where that other room was.

"Shoes. Ya' said ya' needed shoes. I think Farren has a couple of extra pairs. Wolves lose their clothes more than ya' can imagine." Caitlin rummaged in a suitcase and came up with a pair of black running shoes. "Try these on."

Sameen sank down onto a bench at the foot of the bed. It felt so strange to wear clothes again. Shoving her feet into a pair of shoes? The motion was both familiar and completely foreign at the same time.

"How do they fit?" The air elemental sat next to her, a calm, comforting presence amid the chaos.

"They're fine." In truth, she didn't know. How were shoes supposed to feel? She couldn't remember.

"Ya' don't sound sure."

Sameen rested her elbows on her knees and dropped her head into her hands. "I'm not sure of anything. I don't even know if I tied them correctly. I haven't worn clothes or shoes in so long..."

And then Caitlin's arms were around her, and Sameen started to cry. "It's all right, luv. Ye're free now, and ye're part of this family. We won't let anythin' happen to ya.'"

"You don't know the Thirteen."

"Yes. I do." Caitlin's voice faltered, and she swallowed hard. "I met them. Once. They were angry with Fergus. He'd failed three or four times to bind a third element. They summoned him, and he threw me in the boot of his car to drive us...somewhere. It took almost a day." She shuddered. "Air elementals? We can't survive trapped underground or without fresh air. By the time we arrived, I could barely breathe. Fergus dragged me inside this tall, stone castle, and into a ritual space. The Thirteen were there. All of them, and a handful of others wearing black cloaks."

"Victims," Sameen whispered. "Others they bound with their sigil. Like Eli's father. They do whatever the Thirteen command."

Silence stretched between the two women until Sameen shifted so she could take Caitlin's hand. "You don't have to tell me."

Caitlin nodded. "I do. Because ya' need to understand why every one of us will fight for ya'." She carded fingers through her reddish brown curls and stared up at the ceiling. "One of the practitioners—a woman—she used the sigil on Fergus. He knelt at her feet, and when she started chantin', the pain...it was like nothin' I'd ever felt before. They toyed with us for a bit, then threw us in a small, dark cell for what felt like days. I didn't think I'd ever see the sun again."

"How did you get free?" Sameen asked.

"They let us go after Fergus told them he could bring them another dozen elementals." Caitlin braced her hands behind her and leaned back to stretch her legs. "I know those few days were nothin' compared to what ya' went through, Sameen. I've no idea how ya' stayed sane."

"This isn't sanity." She almost laughed, and wasn't that the strangest feeling? "I'm terrified. Twenty-four hours ago, I was blind, I didn't have the strength to stand, and I knew the Thirteen were going to use the sigil to find me any minute. Being able to see? Even if everything's still pretty blurry? It's too much. Too bright. Too many colors. Too much input. It's loud here. All the people. Creaking wood. The wind." Sameen took a deep, shuddering breath. "And then there's Peter. I shouldn't trust him. Or anyone. I don't even know why I'm talking to you. Except you just gave me shoes, and you've been so patient explaining everything to me."

"Matin' is a special kind of magic," Caitlin said quietly. "And our wolves? They feel it in ways we'll never understand. Liam was so overbearin', I told him to feck off a dozen times. And still he risked his life for me. The man should have died. Fergus tortured him. Carved that blasted sigil into his chest. And Liam took a rock and hacked away at his own skin for hours just so he could escape and get to me. Then…there's Peter. He's had a hard time of it."

Caitlin went on to explain all about the fire that led to his and Livie's burns, about how Cade spent months trapped as his wolf because of Mara's sister, and how they'd all found one another again. "There's more. But explainin' how I gave up my life as Caitlin eleven years ago to become someone else…that needs whiskey."

That was what required whiskey?

"Are all families like this?" Sameen asked. "This…much?"

Caitlin chuckled. "I suppose we are a bit over the top now. Ya' get this many wolves together in one house, there's bound to be fights from time to time. Hot tempered, the lot of them. But also the most loyal, loving and protective family ya'd ever want."

"I don't even know who I am. How am I supposed to know what I want?" The question had been playing on repeat in the back of her mind ever since Peter had admitted his wolf had already claimed her.

"When ya' know, ya' know. That's all I can tell ya'. I resisted

Liam for a long time until I couldn't stand to ignore the matin' call. I threw myself off the Cliffs of Moher when I realized the truth. I *died*. In a way. Because if I'd stayed with him all those years ago, Fergus would have killed him, and that would have been the end to me as well."

CHAPTER TWELVE

PETER

His mate walked back into the room under her own power, Caitlin following closely behind. A determination glowed in her pale brown eyes that he hadn't seen before.

This was the real Sameen. Or at least more of her. The beginnings of the woman she would have become had the Thirteen not stolen her from her life and stripped her of all she once was, all she was meant to be.

"Are we ready?" Caitlin asked.

Eli closed the book and passed it to Farren. "As ready as I think we can be for not knowing a bloody thing about Diedre's intentions when she penned these pages."

"Sameen?" Peter approached her slowly, respect in his tone. "Can I have five minutes with you? I won't try to change your mind."

At her nod, Eli jerked his head towards the door. "We'll get set up outside. You two can join us when you're ready."

As soon as they were alone, Peter offered her his hand. Her fingers were cool against his heat, but the touch calmed his wolf enough he thought he might be able to get through this conversation without saying something he'd regret later.

"Sit with me?" she asked. "I still feel like I'm about to fall over."

"I wish we could wait until you were stronger." Sinking down into one of the plusher chairs in the room with Sameen tucked against his side, he quickly added, "I know we have to do this now."

"We do. Because I'm going to lose my nerve soon." His mate pressed closer to him, and Peter took a chance and ran his nose along the curve of her neck. "I like it when you do that. You said...it's a mate thing?"

"It's a wolf thing. Scenting. We operate on instinct. Which is why we also say and do a lot of stupid things."

"Like trying to claim your mate less than a day after meeting her?" The corners of Sameen's lips curved into a half-smile, and it was the most beautiful thing Peter had ever seen. Every new expression, every time she found a bit more of herself, he wanted more.

"Yes." Drawing back slightly, he searched her face. "How well can you see me?"

"Are you asking if I can see your scars?" Sameen reached up and traced some of the worst of the burns along his cheek and down his neck. "Yes. Even up close, things are a little blurry, but I see you, Peter."

"My wolf will always be yours, Sameen. *I* will always be yours. But that doesn't mean you have to be mine. Even if you did one day decide you loved me—or wanted me—mating...it's not ownership. Wolves are possessive. Probably the most possessive creatures on this earth other than vampires. You saw how Farren reacted to the mark on Eli's arm."

Sameen stared down at their joined hands, the differences in their skin tone, in size and shape, and nodded. "I trust you. You make me feel safe and protected and..."

"Loved?"

Her shoulders jerked, and he kicked himself for taking things a step too far. "I don't know what love is. Maybe? I want to be close to you, and I want you to kiss me again."

Peter threaded his fingers through her long locks. "I'll kiss you any time you ask."

She leaned closer and brushed her lips to his. "Give me time." A tear shimmered in the corner of her eye, and Peter dashed it away with his thumb. "After they branded me, I fought them for months. I don't remember much, but I remember having my own thoughts, my own wishes and hopes and dreams. And then...I didn't anymore. I couldn't escape, and every time I resisted, even a little, they'd hurt me."

She shivered, and Peter vowed he'd never let her be cold or afraid or under anyone's control ever again.

"Helping find Mara? Putting an end to them? It terrifies me. But it's the only way I'll ever be able to be...a person again."

"You are—"

"Maybe to you. But not to me. I still feel like this weak shadow of who I might have been. Until I know all my thoughts are my own, until I can make my own decisions, take my own risks, and reclaim what they took from me, I can't promise to stay with you, even if it's the only thing I *know* I want."

Peter cupped her neck so he could touch his forehead to hers. "Whatever you need from me, I'll give you. All you have to do is ask. Ask me to leave you alone or give you space or just back the fuck off. Cade and Liam will tell you...I've been an asshole more often than not this past year. But I want to be better for you. I *will* be better for you. Even if it means I have to let you go."

———

SAMEEN

The wind whipped through the trees at the edge of the vampire's property. She let Peter keep his arm around her waist for the long walk across a perfectly manicured lawn and then into a heavily wooded area where the trees obliterated the moon and the stars and she was almost blind again.

"Peter? I can't see anything." She wasn't proud of the fear in her voice, but the darkness…it terrified her.

He scooped her up into his arms with a grunt of pain. "I can. Wolves have better sight and hearing—even in our human form. Everyone else is just up ahead."

"You won't leave me alone out here, right?" She clung to him, drawing strength from the way his muscles flexed, how very warm he was, and the answering growl as he nuzzled her neck. He wouldn't leave her. Not unless he had no choice.

Sameen wanted to love him—wanted to be *able* to love him, but was this feeling love? This intense need to be close to him? This desire to tell him everything that had happened to her— even the things she couldn't remember—just so he'd understand her a little better? Maybe it was.

After they stopped the Thirteen. After they saved his alpha's mate. After she was free. Then, she'd be able to figure it out.

They emerged from the thick cover of trees into a circle of freshly turned soil lit by the moon. Farren held a large bottle and was pouring something white out onto the dirt at the edges of the space.

"What is that?" Peter asked, setting Sameen down in the center next to Eli. He kept an arm around her waist, and she let him bear much of her weight. She was so tired and ravenously hungry again. She'd forgotten what hunger felt like, and now…the gnawing at her stomach was so intense, it drove much of the fear from her mind—at least temporarily.

"Salt. Once Eli removes the castin' he did to protect Sameen, the salt should stop the Thirteen from takin' her, even if they manage to track her here." Farren finished the salt circle, dropped the bottle into a duffel bag, and brushed off her hands. "How much longer, *mo grá?*"

The practitioner stripped off his shirt and tossed it to his mate. "I'm ready whenever the rest of you lot shift."

"Ewan? Between me and Regulus." Farren tugged her sweater over her head, and the rest of the werewolves—all except Peter—stripped naked right in front of her.

Sameen gaped until Peter cupped her cheek and turned her towards him. "Wolves don't care about being naked, sweetheart. It's too hard to shift wearing clothes."

A hint of jealousy prickled along the back of her neck. "So you just...all the time?"

He kissed her. Only the briefest touch of his lips to hers, and whispered, "Yes. But we only have eyes for our mates." Drawing back, he hesitated. "Do you need me to keep hold of you?"

Eli shook his head. "You can't, Peter. This casting...it's going to be a powerful lot of energy I'm sending into Sameen. If you're touching her, I don't know what it'll do to you."

"I'm not moving to the edge of the circle if that's what you're suggesting." Peter's eyes started to glow, and even with her poor vision and the darkness broken up only by the light of the moon and stars, Sameen could see the anger stiffen his entire body.

"That is exactly what I'm telling you to do."

"Peter," Cade barked. His voice was rougher than it had been inside, and the naked man strode up to them and clapped his hand on Peter's shoulder. "You have to give Eli space to work." At Peter's growl, Cade puffed out his chest. "Don't you think I know how hard this is for you? But you're no good to her if you're dead. So get the fuck back with the rest of us. Eli won't let anything happen to Sameen."

Peter shook off his alpha's hold, surged forward, and

grabbed Sameen in his arms. "Will you let me kiss you?" he asked, his voice ragged and his chest heaving. "Really kiss you."

She nodded, and he tightened his fingers in her hair and claimed her lips. No other word properly described the possessiveness of his kiss. He gave her his promise, his tongue dancing with hers, his teeth nipping gently, and his hard length pressing to her belly.

Memories intact or not, she knew she'd never—ever—been kissed like that before. Her lips throbbed and stung when he finally pulled away. "You'll be able to see me the whole time," he managed. "I'll be right in front of you."

"Promise?" It didn't matter how many times he gave her his word he wouldn't disappear. Sameen still expected to wake up and find out freedom had only been an illusion. A way for the Thirteen to punish her for failing them yet again. Or just her own fractured mind giving up completely.

"I promise." He stripped off his shirt as he stalked away, and she wished it were brighter out here. She needed to see him shift. Needed to know what happened to him—to all of them—when they changed into animal form.

Six humans dropped down to all fours, and then the clearing was full of pops and cracks and gasps of pain. Even with her limited sight, Sameen was in awe of the massive beasts. She could tell them apart. Mostly. Peter was the darkest of the lot. Not quite as bulky as the massive reddish wolf she knew had to be Liam. Cade's pelt was gray with silver streaks, and Farren's wolf was pure white.

Livie was the smallest, and like Peter, she walked with a bit of a limp as they all took their places around the circle.

"Are you ready, Sameen?" Eli asked.

"No. But that's not likely to change. Ever. What...what are you going to do?"

"I'll call on the four elements one at a time," he said as he offered her his hand and led her to the exact center of the circle.

"Then I'll send their power into the mark on my arm. If I'm reading the book correctly, that should be enough to trigger your sigil. You might want to sit or kneel, because I can't imagine this will be comfortable for either of us, and you still look knackered."

Eli helped her down to her knees, and she stared straight ahead. Right at Peter's wolf. God, she hoped this worked.

"I have to remove the casting that hides you first," Eli said quietly. "If the Thirteen try to compel you, I need you to resist for as long as you can."

Eli placed his hand over her heart, and her entire body started to tingle. At first, it was almost pleasant. Like a cool breeze on a warm day. But after a few seconds, his palm glowed hot. When he pulled back, a halo of light burst from her chest like he was tearing out her soul.

Sameen cried out, falling to all fours, and across from her, Peter joined in with a sorrowful howl. Panting through the pain, she focused on the wolf who wanted to be hers.

The air swirled around them, faster and faster, and the humidity spiked, making it hard to breathe as drops of water pelted her hair. The ground rumbled and quaked under her hands and knees, and the mark on her side flared to life. Not from Eli's spell, but from the Thirteen's call.

"No!" she whimpered and curled into a ball. If she couldn't stand up, she couldn't go to them. Couldn't fight anyone who tried to stop her. Peter leapt forward several feet, but stopped at Liam's loud bark. Fire came last, tongues of flames dancing in Eli's hands, and he threw them towards the sky, letting them join with the swirling wind to create a fiery tornado that surrounded the entire group.

Holding out his hands, he shouted into the deafening roar, "Let all who wear this mark know they are not alone!"

She thought she'd been prepared, but when he pressed his

hand to the mark on his arm, pure agony consumed her, driving the Thirteen's magic back with a violent wave of power.

All she could do was scream until she ran out of air. In the second before she inhaled, she sensed another soul in pain. But there was more. Terror. An urgency Sameen knew could only come from one person. Mara. Because though it was faint, a second soul reached out as well. One that echoed Mara in every way, yet was also her complete opposite. Water and fire. Mother and daughter.

Caitlin's voice rang out over the din, though the words didn't make any sense, and a fresh gust of air hit Sameen in the chest. She drew it in, operating on pure instinct, and it flowed through her, a cooling, soothing presence until it found the sigil on her side. Then, Caitlin's element took on a life of its own.

Another scream, this one louder, longer, and more painful escaped Sameen's raw throat, and the air charm followed.

"It's done!" Caitlin shouted. "Hide her again!"

Sameen's chest stuttered, each breath harder than the last. Her body was too weak. Too battered. Had it been enough? Peter's wolf faded into darkness, and silence wrapped her in a warm blanket. One she wasn't sure she'd be able to escape again.

CHAPTER THIRTEEN

PETER

His mate wasn't moving. Sameen lay in the center of the circle, her eyes closed, and her heartbeat so faint, his wolf could barely hear it.

Sprinting to her side, he ran his lupine nose along her neck, begging her to wake up. Eli knelt next to her, and Peter growled a warning when the practitioner touched her.

"Easy, mate. If I don't cast another protection spell, the Thirteen are going to find her."

He couldn't shift back until he knew they were all safe, but fuck, he had to hold her. Laying down next to her, he rested his head on her shoulder.

Eli called all the elements to him, twisting them into a new golden halo he laid over Sameen's side. She shuddered and let out a little whimper.

Peter gave an inquisitive yip, and Eli nodded. "They won't be able to use the sigil against her. Shift and let's get her back to the house. Caitlin? Did the locator charm work?"

"Yes. Mara's northwest of here. Not close. If I had to guess, she's on the Isle of Skye."

Peter let the shift rush over him. The pain took his breath away, but he didn't care. He needed his arms to hold her, and more than anything else, he needed her to hear his voice. Naked and panting, he clawed his way over to his mate and touched her cheek. "Sameen? Can you hear me?"

Her lids fluttered, but she didn't answer him.

"When are we leaving?" Cade asked. "We have to go get Mara. How far is the Isle of Skye?"

Regulus pulled a phone from his pocket, and his fingers flew over the screen. As Peter gathered Sameen into his arms, the vampire nodded. "The plane will be fueled and ready to go in two hours. The flight will take an additional sixty-five minutes. Two SUVs will be at the airstrip when we land."

"Ya' did all of that in the time it took us to shift?" Farren huffed. "Ya' might be helpful to have around, vampire."

Sameen still hadn't moved, and Peter struggled to his feet, ignoring the pain shooting from his shoulder all the way down to his hip. "If Sameen doesn't wake up in two hours, I have to stay with her."

"Everyone goes." Cade tugged on his jeans. "We need her, Peter. She knows the Thirteen like no one else."

"Cade—"

"Watch what you say next, asshole. My mate's out there."

"And mine is right here!"

"Peter?" Sameen's whisper calmed him like nothing else ever could. "What happened? Did it work?"

"It worked, sweetheart."

His mate settled in his arms, resting her head on his shoulder. "Okay. Good. Not doing that again."

Hell no, she wasn't. Peter was going to protect her for the rest of his life and no one was going to use her for that fucking sigil on her side ever again.

"Might I suggest we get back to the mansion?" Regulus said. "We are exposed here, even with the castings the practitioner's son performed."

The group surrounded Peter and Sameen until they passed through the wards Regulus had commissioned many years before to hide his home from any and all magic.

Farren led the way, and when she opened the heavy wooden doors that led into the house, she stopped short. "Where in the bloody hell have ya' been, ya' daft bastard?"

Regulus moved so quickly, Peter only saw a black-clad blur, and the vampire grabbed the old man, fisted his white hair, and bent his head to one side.

"Stop!" Farren shouted. "That's Paddy. He's with us."

"He is trespassing." Regulus's eyes glowed an even darker red, and his normally refined voice took on a rough edge. "No one enters this house without my permission. Particularly not one with magic in him."

"The time for secrets is over," the old man said. "Paddy is here to help."

Cade took his place at Farren's side. "Put him down, Regulus."

"Watch your tone, wolf. This is my house, and I make the rules." Despite his words, Regulus released Paddy, and the practitioner sank down onto the chair he'd been sitting in.

"The storm took yer heart from ya'," he said, turning his pale eyes to Cade. "And the blind found a way to see."

"If you're talking about Sameen, the least you could do is refer to her by name. She just risked everything for us." Peter carried his mate to one of the stately leather couches in front of the hearth and sank down with her still cradled in his arms. His body ached, and had they been any further from the house, he wouldn't have been able to carry her the whole way.

"Ah. Precious one. Old Paddy never knew her name. Never saw her face. Just felt her sufferin'."

"How?" Farren asked. "How did ya' find us? How did ya' get in? And how in the bloody hell did ya' *feel* Sameen's sufferin'? Give us somethin' we can use."

"I'm with Farren," Liam added. The big beta wolf buttoned his flannel shirt and took a seat so he could lace up his boots. "Ya've done nothin' but spout half truths and riddles for months. We know where Mara is, and we're goin' after her."

"Fire consumes, but does not die. In that strength, all hopes lie." Paddy jerked up and staggered over to Peter and Sameen. He put one shaking hand over her eyes. Peter growled a warning, but the old man ignored him—like he wasn't even in the room. *"Newly joined, ya' surely are. By fate and love, even from afar. Yet darkness lurks now deep below, a threat that comes not from a foe. Blood will spill and blood can heal, when given by a heart concealed. Do not despair for darkest night...can be banished by the light."*

Tears stained Sameen's cheeks, and when Paddy straightened with a quiet grunt, her eyelids fluttered, and she turned her head to Peter.

"Who's here?" she whispered, so quietly he had to strain to hear her.

"Old Paddy knows ya', lass. The smart one. Ya' keep yer wits about ya', even though—"

"She knows nothing of the world?" Caitlin asked. "I thought ya' were talkin' about me, Paddy. Back at O'Connor's all these months ago."

"Was I now? Paddy says many things, lass. Rarely do they have only a single meanin'." The old man tapped his nose and shuffled over to Farren. "Paddy can stop fightin' soon. The storm cleared, and Paddy came like he promised ya'."

In Peter's arms, Sameen shifted, trying to sit up, and he wrapped an arm around her shoulders and settled her against him. "That crazy old man has been helping Farren for twenty years. Helped us after Fergus took Liam, told Farren to stop running away from Eli. But we don't know who he truly is or how he knows any of this shit."

"He's...familiar," Sameen said. "I don't know him, but—" She doubled over, pressing her hand to her mark, and across the room, Liam and Farren both winced.

But next to the female alpha, Paddy stood taller. His pale gray eyes clouded over, and his wispy white hair started rising like he'd just stuck his finger in an electric socket.

"*One fire dies so another can burn,*" he said, his voice raspier and definitely not his own. "*The ones in control have not learned. They think Fate guides them to the light, but love's the only path that's right.*"

"Paddy?" Farren grabbed his arm as he started to collapse, and Regulus caught him before he hit the ground. As the vampire lay Paddy out on the sofa across from Peter and Sameen, the man's arm flopped limply to the side, his ratty sweater rising just enough to reveal several curved, black lines on the inside of his wrist.

"Fuck me." Farren pushed the cuff of his sleeve up higher, and the entire room fell silent until Peter remembered Sameen probably couldn't see well enough to know what was going on.

"Paddy has the same sigil as Eli," he whispered in her ear. "Except the circle is broken. That's why he's familiar. Every time the Thirteen controlled someone...you felt Paddy's pain too."

MARA

She woke up with a scream, the lights flickering in the corridor and pain snaking all around her belly.

"*No. Not yet.*"

Despite how broken the other part of her mind was, it had

taken back control while she'd been asleep, and Mara couldn't fight her way free.

"Let me out! This is a contraction! And it's too soon!"

By her estimates, if the Thirteen were advancing her pregnancy a week every day, she'd be six and a half months pregnant. But for all she knew, she could be sleeping for more than twenty-four hours at a time. Or they could have made the spell stronger.

God, she was so hungry. So weak. If they didn't bring her food and water soon, would she even survive long enough to give birth?

She couldn't manage to touch the sigil on her side, not until the intense spasm faded. The fractured part of her mind in control at least remembered some of her Lamaze breathing, and after a few moments, the pain subsided.

Footsteps rushed down the passageway, Celia, Freya, and two of the Thirteen's lackeys entered her cell. Celia pressed hands to Mara's belly, pushing and prodding the baby while Mara could do nothing but sit there with tears running down her cheeks.

"She was further along than we thought," the coven leader said as she yanked the loose dress up and peered at Mara's panties. "Her water hasn't broken yet, but I have to return time to what it should be so we can prepare the ritual space. You know where the conduit is?"

"Yes, Mistress. I could see into her mind when those imbeciles dropped the protection spell. They will bring her right to us."

"When?" Celia asked as she drew a symbol over Mara's belly. A flash of heat burst through her, and the baby kicked, hard, as if she were objecting to anyone touching her mother.

"They have a vampire with them. I doubt they will risk travel before dark."

"You doubt?" Celia rose, Freya following closely, and the two practitioners stepped aside so one of the black-robed minions could set a tray of food in front of Mara. Sandwiches this time. And a glass of greenish liquid. "Be certain. We must be ready to end the wolves if they attempt to rescue her. Use the ancient one if you must," Celia snapped.

"He is no longer beholden to the magic of the creators. He is lost to us."

"Then track the conduit's movements." Celia peered through the bars at Mara, still seated on the mattress, arms cradling her belly, staring at straight ahead. For once, she was relieved that what remained of her sister's consciousness was still in control. They were talking about *ending* her mate. Her family. More tears gathered in her eyes, making everything shimmer. She had to try to use the sigil again. To contact Cade and warn him. To do *something*. He'd already suffered so much because of her and Katerina.

"I promise you, Rachel. I won't let anything happen to your daddy if I can help it." Another kick, softer this time, and the briefest hint of determination flowed from the child she feared she'd never have the chance to know.

With a wave of her hand, Celia murmured a few words in Gaelic, then focused her glowing purple eyes on Mara. "Enjoy your meal, elemental. And drink up. When the moon rises tonight, you and that mangy wolf of yours will be reduced to ash, and your child will be ours forever."

The four of them left her alone, trapped in the small cell with a tray of sandwiches and that disgusting green juice on the small tray. Mara railed against the control her sister's energy had over her body, and as she took the first sip from the plastic cup, she wanted to retch. Spinach and celery and something bitter she feared wasn't natural in the least.

Before the second sandwich was gone, Mara started to feel woozy. Were they drugging her? Why? They could compel her to sleep just by turning off the light.

What does it matter? You're going to die anyway in less than a day.

Her sister's energy fled, leaving Mara in control, but she couldn't hold on to any coherent thought for more than a moment. Even her baby calmed.

The baby. The Thirteen couldn't control the baby with the sigil. *Oh, God. What had they just done to her daughter?*

Mara rocked up to her hands and knees, intending to crawl to the toilet and force herself to vomit up whatever they'd given her, but all of a sudden, she couldn't remember what she'd been about to do.

Absently, her fingers brushed the symbol burned into her side. Pain lanced through her, and for a split second, the fog muddling her thoughts faded. But just as quickly, it rushed back over her, and she sank down onto her side, staring at the rough stone wall outside the bars, and waiting. If only she could remember what she was waiting for.

CHAPTER FOURTEEN

CADE

He couldn't understand why Liam and Farren were being so fucking stupid. The three of them had been arguing for an hour—an hour his mate might not have—rather than listening to him and piling in the cars to head for the vampire's private airfield.

"Paddy knows somethin'," Farren insisted. "I've never seen him like he was today."

"He sure as shit doesn't know how to give a straight answer. *'Fire consumes but doesn't die'*? What the hell is that supposed to mean?" Cade shoved his hands into the pockets of his jeans—he still hadn't bothered to put on a shirt—and his wedding ring hanging from the chain around his neck caught the light. If he didn't get to his mate soon, he'd lose her forever, and then he'd lose himself.

"I think he means Mara's stronger because she has two elements in her," Caitlin offered, stifling a yawn. *"In that strength all hope lies.'* Or somethin' like that."

"Aye. Ya' understand old Paddy now." The elderly man's whisper startled them all, and Cade whirled around, grabbed him by the arms, and hauled him up to sitting. He wanted to shake Paddy. Hard enough to rattle some sense loose, but given how frail the soothsayer appeared, Cade would probably crush him instead.

"Explain the rest," he growled. "We need to get to Mara."

Paddy shook his head and pointed to one of the windows along the far wall. "Day breaks. There's no winnin' without the blood of the stone."

"The blood of the stone—holy fuck, old man. What do you know about that?"

The sight of one who has not seen will find the blood of the stone.

The words of the dying practitioner in the dungeon haunted Cade every waking minute. The only way they'd find Mara. They all agreed the *'one who has not seen'* had to be Peter's mate, but the blood of the stone? What the hell was that?

Before Paddy could answer, Regulus streaked across the room and slammed his hand down on a button on the wall. Several loud *thunks* reverberated throughout the house, and Sameen yelped softly from where she'd been dozing in Peter's arms.

"It's okay, sweetheart," Peter murmured. "Just Regulus making sure the house is protected from the sun."

"The ancient one is right," the vampire said, his voice strained as he rested his hand on Ewan's shoulder. The young, newly made vampire looked downright exhausted, his face ashen and a pained expression twisting his features. "Dawn approaches rapidly, and we do not know how long the magic that allows me to walk in the sun will last. The youngling has no such boon, and he—more than I—needs to go to ground to rest. We will leave at dusk."

"Hell, no." Cade strode over to the vampire and drew up to

his full height. "They could be torturing Mara right now. Killing her. We can't wait."

The pure agony of knowing he couldn't help his mate, couldn't do a damn thing without Regulus's plane, without his pack, ate away at him, making him feel less and less like an alpha every second.

"Cade?" Eli staggered to his feet, and the strain in his voice mirrored his posture. "That casting to locate Mara was the hardest thing I've ever done. I need to rest if I'm going to be any help at all freeing her."

"We're all exhausted," Farren added. "We're no use to her if we're too tired to shift or even stand up."

"And what if they kill her before tonight?" Cade ran a hand through his shaggy locks, staring up at the ceiling and letting out a mournful howl. "She's out there, suffering. And we're supposed to what? Sleep? Under thousand thread-count sheets in a fucking mansion while she's probably in some dungeon two hundred miles away, alone and in pain?"

Eli snagged the practitioner's book from the table and flipped it open. "Yes. Because look at these pages. After that blasted sigil inked itself on my arm, the symbols here started to make sense."

Cade stared at the yellowing parchment. The symbols of the four elements surrounded a rough sketch of a woman standing on the top of a mountain. Chains bound her arms wide, and above her head, a waxing moon.

The moon had set only a few minutes ago, and Cade instinctively *knew* that its fullness would match that of the drawing tonight. Not long after midnight.

The next page showed the same woman, no longer standing but slumped in the chains, with the symbol they'd all come to associate with spirit—the triskele, three distinct sets of swirls arranged around a center point—above her head.

"They're going to perform the ceremony tonight." The book

slipped from Cade's hands, and Eli caught it, then passed it to Farren, who scanned the page and handed the tome to Peter. "Isn't that all the more reason to go now? What if we leave at dusk and we're wrong about where they're holding her? We'll lose any chance to regroup and try again."

Paddy shook his head. "Ya' were only meant to have one chance." He pulled up his sleeve to reveal the sigil inked on his skin. Pressing a frail, bony finger to the broken part of the circle, he shuddered. "*Old Paddy has seen many an end. Over and under, again and again. Ne're can water, earth, nor air, find the path without their pair. True love's flame can never die, but not all is seen with the eye. On this night he holds no fear, for victory comes when truth is clear.*"

"What the bloody fuck is that supposed to mean?" Farren asked. "Ye're goin' to die?" She shook her head. "No. I won't let ya'."

"Ya' do not have a choice, lass. This is the way." Paddy's wrinkled lips curved slightly, showing at least three missing teeth before turning to Cade. "Never will be whole," he said and tapped his nose, "until evil leaves this world. Paddy sees now. Ya' aren't alone. None of ya' are."

With that, he rose, swayed on his feet, and shuffled towards the stairs. "Paddy knows where to go." Halfway to the second floor, he added, "To bed."

Cade sank down on the couch the old man had been lying on and dropped his head into his hands. "Fine. But we're leaving the second it's dark enough for Regulus and Ewan to be safe."

Farren took Eli's arm, and Peter helped Sameen to her feet. Everyone headed for their rooms until only Liam remained.

"I trust ye're not goin' to boost one of the vampire's cars and try to *drive* to Skye, right?"

"I'd crash before I made it five miles." Cade pushed up with a groan. "I don't remember the last time I slept."

"My Caitlin can help with that." Liam slung an arm around

Cade's shoulders and guided him towards the stairs. Cade bristled at the idea, but Liam let out a low growl. Almost challenging. "Ya' keep sayin' that family sticks, Cade. But that's not all family does. We trust one another. And we ask for help when we need it. Ya' taught all of us that...more than once over the past year. Ye're knackered, and we need to be at our best when we go up against those bastards. Let me get Caitlin for ya'."

Though the idea of anyone drugging or charming him ever again left Cade with an icy ball of fear sinking in his gut, his beta was right. Without rest, he'd fail his mate, and then...he'd lose everything.

SAMEEN

She was starting to find her bearings. The room Peter brought her to was across from Farren's. Her whole body ached from exhaustion and whatever Eli's casting had done to her, and the Thirteen's brand felt raw. With every step, her t-shirt rubbed over the skin, sending sparks of pain all through her.

Peter stood awkwardly by the bed as Sameen untied her shoes. "I can sleep in the chair in the corner."

Her head snapped up, so quickly, the room spun around her. "Wh-what?"

"You're exhausted, sweetheart." He cupped her cheek and skated his thumb just under her eye. "I would spend every single second next to you if I could. But you need to rest."

"I want you to hold me." Six words. Words she wasn't sure she could say until they came out of her mouth. She squinted up at him in the dim light from the bedside lamp. "You make me feel safe." With a shiver, she wobbled to her feet. "I just need a minute."

In the bathroom, she took care of her needs and pointedly refused to look at her reflection in the mirror. Ever since the vampire had given her back some of her sight, she'd tried to remember what she looked like. And now that she had the chance to find out, she was too scared to raise her eyes.

Quickly, she stripped out of the borrowed sweater and yoga pants and folded them neatly, needing Peter's arms around her, his warmth, his strength.

Returning to the bedroom, she gaped. Flames flickered in a gas fireplace built into the wall, heating the room and Peter sat on the bed, still fully clothed.

"These old mansions are drafty as fuck," he said when she burrowed under the covers. "Do you want an extra blanket too?"

"No. Just you." For the hour or so the rest of the group had been fighting, she'd slept in his arms, and she'd found a measure of peace she ached to have again. Now, even this short distance between them was too much.

He started to climb into bed, and Sameen stopped him with her hand to his chest. "You don't have to sleep in your clothes, Peter."

"You're not ready—"

"Let me be the judge of what I'm ready for." With a huff, she reached for the buttons on his flannel shirt. "I just watched you strip and shift into a wolf. And when you found me, we were both naked, remember? I'm not going to have sex with you, but...I want to feel your skin. Please?"

He swallowed hard enough she could hear it. "It's not...pretty."

"What isn't? Your body?" Sameen pulled up the hem of her t-shirt. "What about this? I'll always have this, Peter. Even if we...win. Even if the Thirteen are dead and gone, they branded me. And I can't destroy it. Can't scratch it off of me like Liam did. Can't heal a part of it like Farren. If I didn't think we might need it again to find Mara, I'd beg you for a knife and cut it to break their control, but even if I did...the mark won't ever go away. So tell me why you're so ashamed of your scars, when you don't seem to care about mine?"

"I wasn't strong enough," he spat. "Shit." Jerking up, he started to pace. "This fire elemental who came after Cade—Mara's sister—she used a charm to stop us from shifting. Wolves heal quickly. Broken bones, cuts, bruises...once we shift, they go away. We don't carry diseases, don't ever get sick. But that fucking charm stopped me and Livie from shifting for days. Cade...she kept him as his wolf for almost a year. That's why Livie and I aren't...whole."

"Whole?" She wriggled until she was sitting up, her back against the headboard. This was *not* a conversation she wanted to have lying down. "So, because you were burned, you're not whole? Then what does that make me? I have *their sigil* branded on me. It's never going to go away. Not even if we defeat them. You're talking about your scars like they define you. If so, I'll never be more than their possession." The first tears spilled onto her cheeks, and she swiped them away, more angry than she'd ever been—that she could remember.

"Sameen, shit. I'm sorry." He knelt on the bed, too far away for her to reach, and scrubbed his hands up and down his thighs. "You're not their possession. You're smart and beautiful and when you get angry, your personality..." A sound that might have been a laugh escaped his lips, and he shook his head. "You told me earlier that you didn't know who you were anymore. Who you were supposed to be. Well, I see that woman now. Telling me I'm a fucking idiot who needs to stop feeling so sorry for myself and grow a pair."

She gaped at him, shocked not only at her own brazenness, but at how quickly he'd taken her words to heart and managed to help her see her own truth in addition to his. "So take off your shirt," she said. "Pants too. And hold me."

He only hesitated for a moment before grabbing the hem of his shirt and yanking it over his head. Even from a few feet away, even with her eyes only partially healed, she could see the reddish raised patches of skin. He grunted as he got to his feet and swore softly, lifting his left leg to step out of his jeans. "Broke my hip in the fire," he said, refusing to look at her as he got under the covers. "Dislocated my shoulder and fractured my collarbone. We were on the run. Two of us trapped in wolf form, injured. Wasn't like we could just find a doctor. Or a vet. Not with Katerina after us. Liam stole a van and drove us to Canada, and once Livie and I could shift back, we left for Ireland."

"Come here," Sameen said. He scooted closer, and she ran her fingers over his left arm, across his chest, and all the way up his neck. "All I feel is you."

"I couldn't even carry you back here after Eli cast that protection spell this morning." The words escaped like he was admitting his greatest shame. "Liam had to do it. You're my mate. I should be able to take care of you, and I can't."

"You carried me earlier." The thought of being his mate didn't scare her as much as it had just a few hours ago, but this wasn't the time to figure out why. He needed her now, and after everything he'd done, how he'd protected her, given her back her choices, a piece of herself she thought she'd lost forever, all she wanted was for Peter to see himself the way she saw him.

"For all of a quarter mile."

Sameen snuggled against his chest, relishing his warmth and letting her legs tangle with his. The idea of taking things further terrified her, but this? This felt...right. "It doesn't matter how far you can or can't carry me," she said as she let her eyes drift closed and breathed in his scent. "You gave me something I didn't even know I needed."

"What?"

"The chance to find myself again." Resting her hand over his heart, she relished in its steady beat. "I haven't yet. Not completely. But...I'm getting there."

CHAPTER FIFTEEN

PETER

He was burning. Trapped under a large wooden beam, the sound of screaming all around him. His wolf howled, and he heard Liam's weak voice somewhere behind him. "Livie!"

The female wolf whined, and Shawn called her name. "I'm coming, Liv!"

"Peter. Fuck me. Hang on." The tall, beta wolf stood over him, naked and covered in soot and bloody scratches. The pain etched on Liam's face as he hefted burning wooden beams and pieces of concrete off Peter made him whine and whimper, but Liam would be able to shift as soon as he'd freed Peter and heal any injury.

The left side of his body felt like it had been burnt to a crisp by the time the debris had been cleared away, and Peter scrambled up on all fours, his wolf still in control, desperate to get away from the flames before he shifted back into a man.

"To the water," Liam ordered. "Don't stop. She won't be able to hurt ya' there. I have to find Cade!"

Peter tried to run, but all he managed was a slow, agonizing limp. The bay was only two blocks west. He could make it.

Shawn caught up with him at the edge of the water, carrying his unconscious mate in his arms, and splashed into the frigid depths alongside Peter.

The shock made him lose his breath. No. If he blacked out, he'd drown. In a panic, he tried to swim back to shore, but his head sunk below the water. He howled, knowing Shawn was close by, but his wolf was in so much pain, he wasn't thinking. The water rushed into his lungs. So much. *Can't breathe.*

"Peter!"

Soft hands framed his face. Delicate fingers fluttered over his cheeks. His mate. She smelled like home. Sweet and fresh and very much his.

Sameen.

He couldn't form words. Halfway between the nightmare and reality, he might as well still have been in wolf form for all the control he had over his body.

"Peter, look at me." Her voice brought him back. The demand. The urgency. The hint of fear. He couldn't let her be afraid. Ever. Not when he had the power to soothe her.

Wrapping his arms around her, he buried his face in her neck. "Bad dream," he managed.

"It sounded like you were choking."

"Drowning." He shuddered, and Sameen kissed his burned and mangled shoulder. Again, and again, she followed the scars up his neck, and damn if she didn't kiss the exact spot that could —when the moon was full—seal their bond. It wasn't required. At least not according to Liam. He and Caitlin had bonded slowly, over the weeks they spent together in Dublin years ago. Would it work the same with Sameen?

Peter wasn't born a wolf like Cade, Liam, and Livie. He'd

been bitten as a teenager. That made him weaker than the others. Guaranteed he'd never be an alpha—not that he'd ever wanted to be.

"Tell me?" she asked. Settling closer to him, her forehead touching his, she played with his hair. It had gotten too long these past months, but if Sameen liked it this way, he'd keep it.

"It's not a story you want to hear, sweetheart." Peter checked the bedside clock. Regulus had outfitted the mansion with every modern convenience, yet also seemed to obsess over antiques. And timepieces. In one of the bureau drawers, Peter had found a tray of twenty-five vintage watches, each probably worth more than the second-hand Audi he'd lusted after back in Seattle. The one he'd been about to buy just before Cade ordered him to Ireland.

"You know what happened to me," she whispered. "Some of it, anyway."

Shit. He was complaining about *his* pain? Telling her his story was too terrible to tell when she'd been trapped in her own body for years, had lost her sight when they'd forbidden her from blinking, and couldn't even remember her last name?

"I'm sorry, Sameen. That was insensitive as fuck of me."

"No." His mate reached over and stroked her hand down his chest to his stomach. "Pain isn't something you can compare."

"The hell it isn't. You were their prisoner for more than twelve years."

"And I'm not pregnant and about to give birth. You think what I went through is worse than what Mara's dealing with? I felt her, Peter. Her and the baby. She's so scared. She's convinced she's going to die and she's completely alone."

A tear fell, landing on Peter's shoulder, and Sameen choked back a sob.

"That's what they do. They kill elementals to take their power. They keep their prisoners alone. Confined. Controlled. Not just their bodies, but their minds too."

"Their minds?"

"If Celia wanted, she could make Mara believe Cade was her enemy. Eli's father? I knew him. Or...I knew of him. Even though I couldn't speak or see, I could hear. One time, he begged them to kill him. A few words from Celia and he told her he wanted to live. To serve her until his last breath."

"Fuck. Except...he fought her. Farren destroyed his sigil, and he's free now."

"Destroyed it?" Sameen sat up, her hand pressing to her stomach. "How? Can she do the same thing for me? Once we know we don't need it to find Mara anymore?"

The hair on the back of Peter's neck stood on end, and he shook his head. "No. Absolutely not. Farren took a chunk out of his side, and since it all happened on the full moon, he turned. His wolf ran away when we destroyed the compound, and we haven't seen him since."

The shock and horror on Sameen's face made Peter's heart skip a beat. If he could, he'd move heaven and earth to take away her pain. Her scars. But nothing could erase the past twelve years. Or for him, the past twelve months.

"They'll never stop hunting me," she said quietly when Peter urged her back down next to him. "They know I'm alive, Peter. In the circle? When Eli removed the protection spell? I felt them. Celia's magic...it's stronger than all of the others, and she called to me. I resisted, but I don't know that I'm strong enough to do it again."

A low growl rumbled in Peter's chest, and he pulled her closer, caging her in his arms and pressing his lips to hers. He poured everything he was into that kiss, and when Sameen yielded to the slightest flick of his tongue and opened to him, the growl turned deeper, almost desperate.

He wanted her. Needed her. Sameen rolled on top of him, and her nipples pebbled under the thin t-shirt. Peter slid his hand along her waist to her hip until he found the smooth, supple skin of her thigh. She shivered, but this time, it wasn't from the cold. He scented her arousal, her need, but through their tenuous bond came a burst of fear. She wasn't ready for this yet. Not after everything she'd been through.

"Enough," he panted, breaking off the kiss and willing his cock to calm the fuck down. "For now."

Sameen's eyes were bright, her parted lips swollen, and she pressed her hand to her heart. "You stopped. Why did you stop?"

"Because if we do this, Sameen, we do this right. And that means nothing happens you aren't completely ready for. We have time. Once we get Mara back, we'll have the rest of our lives." He sealed his promise with a gentler, almost chaste kiss, and tucked the blankets around them. "We still have a couple of hours before Cade starts getting pissy and wakes everyone up. Sleep a little longer with me?"

"I'll try." Sadness tinged her tone, but when he cupped her cheek and asked her what was wrong, she forced a smile. "I want the chance for a life, Peter. With you."

He kissed the top of her head as she let out a little sigh and relaxed against him.

Oh, you'll have your life, sweetheart. Because I'll die before I let them hurt you again.

PETER WASN'T WRONG. Just under two hours later, Cade pounded on the bedroom door. "We're leaving in thirty minutes," he called. A few seconds later, he repeated the same exact words across the hall.

"We know, ya' arse. Do ya' think we're faffin' about in here? We've been ready for an hour," Farren snapped. Her door slammed, and Cade stomped towards the stairs muttering to himself.

Sameen sat up and swung her legs over the side of the bed. "Will you do something for me?" she asked, her voice so quiet, he could barely hear her.

"Anything." He rounded the bed and knelt in front of her, his hands on her bare thighs.

"Cut my hair." Gathering the long locks in her hand, she draped her tresses over her shoulder so the ends brushed Peter's fingers. "When they took me, I think…it only reached my shoulders. Twelve years. I had no control over my body. This…I know it's a little thing. Something I shouldn't even think about right now. But before I have to face them…"

"Shhh, sweetheart. If you want me to cut your hair, I'll cut your hair."

Peter led her into the bathroom and flipped on the light, then frowned when Sameen turned away from the mirror. "What's wrong?"

"I…I don't know what I look like," she whispered. "I haven't looked. Not once."

Peter framed her face with his hands and brushed a light kiss to her lips. "You're beautiful."

"It's not that…" She kept her gaze focused on his chest, like she thought he'd be angry or disappointed with her. "I kept hoping I'd remember. That who I was…would come back to me. But last night, I realized I didn't care. Who I was isn't important. I need to figure out who I am."

His mate was so much more than beautiful. She was brave. Strong. And so fucking intelligent and down to earth he couldn't believe she was real. After all she'd been through, to be able to stand in front of him half naked and give him so much of her trust…

"You're the bravest person I've ever met," he said, taking her hands and linking their fingers. "You're willing to risk your own life to help people you didn't know existed two days ago. And you told me off this morning like you knew *exactly* who you were and what you wanted."

Her cheeks flushed, and she stammered out an apology, but Peter silenced her with a kiss.

"Sameen, you standing up for yourself? That was the sexiest damn thing I've ever seen. And you weren't wrong. I deserved every word. And probably a lot more."

His mate almost smiled. "I wish I had your confidence."

With a snort, Peter dropped her hands and started rummaging in the bathroom drawers until he found a pair of scissors. "When I could finally shift back after the fire? I could barely figure out how to make my tongue work. Couldn't stand up. Couldn't move my left arm at all. I was so pissed. And scared. Wolves...we're fast. Strong. The next full moon? I couldn't run. We were at Liam's family estate outside of Dublin, and me and Livie? We were stuck inside. At least Livie could shift. I was too scared to try. What if I got stuck again? What if I never came back?"

Peter turned Sameen to the side, making sure she didn't have to face the mirror, and gathered her hair in his hands, suddenly terrified he was going to cut too much or too little and shit. She could hate it.

"That confidence you think you see? It's an act. Hell, I think it's an act with most people. Cade's an alpha. He was born to lead. It's in his blood. And the second Mara was taken? He was just as broken as the rest of us."

Sameen peered over her shoulder. "That's how I feel. Broken. The Thirteen broke me in every way they could. And some they didn't even intend. So much so, I don't remember what it was like to be...whole."

"No one's whole, Sameen. We like to think we are, but we're not. Everyone's broken in different ways." Peter took the chance to press a kiss to her cheek, then picked up the scissors. "How short do you want to go?"

CHAPTER SIXTEEN

The black leather jacket wasn't anywhere near as comfortable as the soft t-shirt and sweater she'd worn the previous day. Every piece of clothing she had on now was designed for battle. Black pants that clung to her slight curves, a fitted gray tank top, and the jacket all weighed her down, but at least her hair felt lighter.

After Peter had sliced off a good ten inches, she'd combed her fingers through her thick locks, trying to remember how she used to wear it. Before the Thirteen had taken her life away. Back when she'd been her own person. With her eyes closed, muscle memory had taken over, and she'd separated her hair into three sections, crafting a perfect french braid in just a few minutes.

"Peter?" she called. He'd retreated to the bedroom to give her some privacy, but came running.

"Is something wrong?"

"No. I just… I need a rubber band. Or a hair tie."

He pulled open drawer after drawer. "I don't want to know why every bathroom in this place has a full supply of makeup, 'feminine products,' and enough condoms for an army base on leave for the first time in a year."

"*Every* bathroom?" She almost lost her grip on the end of the braid.

"Yep. I asked Liam, Caitlin, and Livie. They're all weirded out by it too. I've only known Regulus for a couple of years, but he's never breathed a word about *female* companionship. Here you go." Peter pressed a wrapped elastic band into her palm, and she twisted it like she'd done so every day of her life.

"Well?" she asked. "Did I do it right?"

With a chuckle, Peter cupped her cheek. "You're asking the wrong guy. Liam would be the better one. I offered to cut his hair once when we were hiding out in Dublin after Cade was taken, and...it didn't go over well. The man is obsessed with finding the perfect curl cream. But don't tell Caitlin. She thinks he just wakes up that pretty every morning."

Sameen stifled her laugh, but all too quickly, fear dashed away the sense of belonging. Of family. When Eli had dropped the protection spell, she'd felt Celia. Felt the sigil on her side burn. Reminding her she'd never be truly free. Not unless the Thirteen were dead and gone. She'd even wondered if the practitioners had somehow known she'd be unprotected. Celia's calling had been almost immediate. The werewolves—everyone in this house, really—were confident they could put an end to the Thirteen, save Mara and the baby, *and* make sure Sameen would always be free if they worked together, but her doubts crept closer every minute.

"Sweetheart? What's wrong? I may not know anything about hair, but...you're beautiful. You were gorgeous before, but this..." Peter skimmed his fingers over the braid, careful not to mess it up. "It's perfect. It's you. In every way."

His reassurance brought a smile to her lips, even if she

couldn't quell her fears for long. She'd reclaimed a small piece of herself. One she hoped she'd never lose again.

PETER

Regulus opened the cabin door, and a stiff breeze swirled around them. The Isle of Skye was only barely accessible by car, and large parts of the island had no cell service or even paved roads.

The plane had touched down in a clearing at the base of a small mountain where Caitlin believed Mara was being held. "It should be less than a fifteen minute drive," Regulus said. "But wait here until I ensure the men I hired to bring us the SUVs do not speak of what they see here tonight."

Sameen peered up at Peter. "What does he mean?"

"Vampires can affect people's thoughts. Control their minds," Peter replied. "Regulus can cause them to forget everything so no one knows where we came from, how we got here..."

"Is he...would he ever...?" his mate asked, her eyes wide.

"No. Regulus owes me a life debt. He wouldn't. Not to us. Any of us."

From the way Sameen fiddled with the hem of the black jacket Farren had loaned her, she wasn't reassured.

The vampire returned to the plane and nodded. "The drivers will wait here with the pilot. Assuming we survive this night. If not, my *glamour* will fade, and they will eventually regain use of their faculties."

Dividing themselves between the two SUVs, Farren, Eli, Liam, Caitlin, Regulus, and Ewan in one, and Peter, Sameen, Cade, Livie, Paddy, and Tierney in the other, they set off with Caitlin directing them.

Cade's phone buzzed, and he put it on speaker. "How much

longer?" he asked.

"Another five kilometers, at most," Caitlin said. "The map shows a pretty steep climb ahead, so we should park maybe halfway up and go on foot the rest of the way."

Regulus, whose vision was better than anyone else's, agreed. "There is a large stone structure on the peak of that cliff. With light emanating from it. Weak, but most definitely present."

"When we get close," Eli said, "it's possible they'll sense me. My magic. And Sameen's mark."

Next to Peter, Sameen shuddered. "I can feel them. They'll know I'm here. If they don't already."

"But the protection charm..." Peter tightened his arm around his mate's shoulders, his wolf demanding to be freed. "Eli, tell me it'll keep working."

"It should stop their magic from controlling her. Should. But that mark is more powerful than any I've ever felt, and I can't promise everything won't go sideways when we get there."

The urge to leap out of the SUV with Sameen and carry her back to Glasgow, back to the United States even, surged through Peter. Fuck. He couldn't lose her. Not now. "I won't let anything happen to you, sweetheart. I promise."

"Don't." Sameen peered up at him, her eyes straining to focus and uncertainty marring her delicate features. "Don't make promises you can't keep. This is my one chance to be free of them, and I'll fight as hard and as long as I can to remain so. But Mara is the only one who truly matters tonight. If they go through with their plan—if they can channel the elements in me, in Mara, in any other prisoners they've captured over the years—and create Spirit..." She shook her head. "It'll be the end of everything."

The moon was close. Peter could feel its impending rise, and from the seat behind them, Paddy moaned. "*It has begun. Fire sleeps but not by choice. Water fights but has no voice. Earth and air must once more pair, or all will soon despair.*"

Cade slammed his hand down on the dashboard. "What the fuck does that mean, old man? We're about to go fight for our lives, for *Mara's* life, for the life of our *child*, and you still can't manage to give us a straight answer?"

"Tis not the way Paddy was made."

"What are ya' talkin' about?" Farren asked over the line. "Made? Ya' were born, weren't ya'?"

The elderly man's chuckle set Peter's nerves on edge. Cade was right. This close to a group of practitioners who could kill them all with just a few words and Paddy thought it was time to joke around?

"Tis a fair question. And one ya' should have asked long ago."

Liam growled and swore quietly from the other car. "Can we focus on what we're about to do? Who the hell cares where Paddy came from? His nonsense isn't goin' to save Mara."

"Do not speak of what you do not know," Paddy snapped. "Not every truth is right. Not every lie is wrong. Salvation comes from strength of heart, not of body."

"Enough!" Regulus shouted. The vampire so rarely displayed any emotion at all, everyone fell silent. "Park up ahead. Young one, you are to shift and remain as your wolf for as long as you can. Magic has more power over the human form than animal. If I fall, you will have only one to look to, and for that, I am sorry."

"If they end ya'," Ewan replied, his voice cracking, "how am I supposed to survive?"

"Did ya' forget I was here?" Farren huffed. "I'm still yer alpha."

"But ya' don't know anythin' about the hunger. About how to handle it when all ya' want is blood and ye're afraid ye're goin' to attack those ya' love most in this world."

"This. Is. Not. The. Time." Cade's voice took on a hint of his wolf as Livie and Regulus pulled the SUVs off to the side of the road. "Once Mara's safe, you can fight all you want. Not before."

Sameen let Peter help her out of the car, but then wrapped her arms tightly around herself and stared up the hill. The stone building looked to be three stories tall, and now that they were closer, Peter could see lights flickering from the top floor.

"Are you all right?" he asked his mate. He'd have to shift soon, and once he did, he wouldn't be able to talk to her. Not in a way she could understand.

With a shake of her head, she replied, "I don't know. I can feel them. The Thirteen. Or what's left of them. They're not as strong as they were before."

Peter snorted. "I should hope not. We killed five of them." That should have brought her some comfort, but she swiped at her eyes, and a tear glistened on the back of her hand.

"Not Celia. She was always the strongest. This is *her* mark. The others can use it when she allows, but she has more power than all of the rest put together. I've always known...since the day they took me...that she would be the one to end me."

"No. I won't let that happen," Peter snarled. "I will die before I let them touch you. Hurt you in any way."

"Peter." Sameen swallowed a sob. "Please..."

"Time to shift," Cade said, interrupting them. "Now."

Grabbing his mate and hauling her against him, Peter kissed her, pouring all of his love, every promise he'd made and all the ones he hadn't yet had the chance to offer her into this one, passionate act. "I love you, Sameen. No matter what happens, know that I love you."

He pulled off his shirt, shed his jeans and boots, and dropped down to all fours. Sameen knelt next to him, her hand on his shoulder as he let his bones break. She wasn't afraid of him. Wasn't shocked or disgusted by the shift, by the way his fur sprouted all over his body, didn't even blink when his tail lengthened and his ears sharpened into points.

He sat up, panting, and she wrapped her arms around him, burying her face against his neck and sobbing as the other wolves came to stand around them, one by one. Cade barked softly, the order to move unmistakable, and Sameen tightened her hold and whispered in his ear. "You saved me, Peter. Never forget...you saved me."

And then she released him. Caitlin and Eli flanked her, and Cade started to run, just as a woman's scream pierced the night air.

———

SAMEEN

She should have told him. Been faster. Or braver. So many times over the past few hours, she'd almost worked up the courage, and now, it was too late.

Peter was her mate. Even though she couldn't remember her last name, her childhood, or tell him what foods she liked, her favorite color...she knew they were meant to be together. Or, would have been, had it not been for the Thirteen and their plan to destroy her.

Why hadn't she confessed just how intensely she felt Celia's magic calling to her through the brand? Had she put them all in terrible danger?

Caitlin called on the power of her air, and a strong current propelled the three of them forward twice as fast as they would have been able to run. Eli used his elements to conjure a thick fog that wrapped around the massive stone structure and rolled down the hill in waves. Regulus kept pace with them easily, his enhanced speed probably making their sprint seem like a slow jog, and every few moments, he cast a glance in Sameen's direction, his brows furrowed.

He could read minds. He'd told her so right after he'd given her his blood. Had the connection waned? Or could he still sense her thoughts? If so...maybe he could help her.

The sigil, which had started to pulse with power the moment they'd exited the SUV, now burned, so hot she wasn't sure she could stop from crying out much longer. Celia knew she was close, and Sameen feared even Eli's protection charm wouldn't be enough to save her.

Fight. You have a life now. People you care about.

Focusing on Peter, who ran just ahead of her, close enough a single leap would bring him back to her side, she kept repeating those words over and over again.

The sigil was so hot now, only the years of unending agony she'd endured at the Thirteen's hands allowed her to remain upright and semi-functional. She was used to pain. Used to fighting through it, banishing it to the deepest recesses of her mind—when they'd allowed her that control—and she'd continue to do so for as long as she could.

A wave of powerful magic washed over her, too much for her to keep fighting, and she drew in a sharp breath.

"It is time for you to fulfill your destiny." Freya—Celia's favorite and the second strongest practitioner of the bunch—laughed in Sameen's head. Freya's idea of fun had always been to torture the poor, paralyzed conduit. To tease her with food, to offer freedom if only Sameen asked for it. But trapped in her own body, she'd been unable to move or speak, and Freya had known it.

"What's wrong?" Caitlin asked when Sameen stumbled.

"I can feel them. We don't have much time." The words weren't hers. Not the ones she wanted to say, though that made them no less true. Freya invaded her mind, her magic spreading all through Sameen's body until the witch could control every-thing she said or did. Even her thoughts, though Freya seemed to care little about those at the moment.

"You pathetic thing. Did you think you could escape us? You have always been ours."

"Please," Sameen begged. *"Don't do this. Let Mara and the wolves*

go. I know I failed you. But I won't this time. I can still be your conduit. You only need to take the elements from me and channel them."

Freya laughed, the sound making Sameen's stomach twist into a knot. *"Your only purpose is to bring us the elemental's mate and the practitioner's son. And to give up all that we put inside you."*

Deliver Cade to the Thirteen? No. She couldn't. She wouldn't. She'd find a way to end her own life first. She ached to call out for Regulus, but if she did, Freya would know. If only he'd look over at her again. See what must be pure agony in her eyes.

Another scream—this one weaker and filled with pain—came from inside the stone structure, and just ahead of them, Cade snarled.

"That's Mara," Caitlin reached for Sameen, clutching her hand tightly. "They're hurting her."

The rest of the wolves answered the alpha, communicating in a language of quiet yips and barks Sameen couldn't understand.

"They're making a plan. Splitting up. We're to do the same. Stay with Regulus and Peter and Eli. I'm going with Liam. They can scent more than just the eight practitioners in there."

"Novitiates," Regulus spat. "Trainees. When they held me captive, the novitiates wore light purple robes. Full-fledged practitioners wore dark purple. But even those with new magic can be deadly. Beware."

Fire, water, and air fought for dominance inside Sameen, and she doubled over, pulling away from Caitlin. Regulus caught her elbow, and when she stared up at him, the vampire hissed and bared his fangs.

"You are in their thrall."

"No!" Freya commanded Sameen's body, trying to free her from the vampire's grip, but his fingers were stronger than steel, and he threw her over his shoulder and raced away from the rest of the group.

"Do not deviate from the plan," he called to Caitlin and Eli.

The magic flowing through the sigil surged even stronger, and the practitioner called to the fire elements deep inside Sameen, chanting in Gaelic until Sameen's hands started to glow red hot.

"No! Please don't do this!"

The witch didn't respond, and when smoke wafted from her fingers, the vampire cursed and threw her down to the ground, robbing her of her ability to breathe from the impact.

"You think to burn me, witch? To take the mind of one so pure? Think again."

Peter's wolf growled, and even with Freya's magic controlling her and the fire blistering her fingers, Sameen held on to the thinnest shred of her own sanity. Regulus would help her. Stop her from hurting anyone else. And Peter would come.

"Kill me," she begged the vampire without words, but he gave her an almost imperceptible shake of his head and bared his fangs. *"They'll make me hurt Peter. Hurt everyone. They want Cade and Eli!"*

"You have said enough, conduit," Freya snarled, and coherent thoughts fled. Fragments, words, pleas ran through her mind, but nothing made sense and she was still burning.

Regulus advanced on her, a gleam in his blood red eyes, but as he reached for her, flames shot from her hands and she screamed. He leapt back, the fire licking the hem of his leather coat.

Sameen's muscles locked tight, the seizure taking hold of her as Peter—his wolf almost silent—sailed over a burning patch of grass to connect solidly with the vampire's chest.

"You pathetic, weak thing. We should have put an end to you long ago. Get up!"

She couldn't. Not until the seizure ended, but Freya didn't

care, and the magic drew a scream from her throat as every fiber of her being cried out in pain.

Regulus tossed Peter's wolf aside like he weighed nothing at all, and Peter fell with a pained yelp. When he tried to get up, his left front leg collapsed under his weight.

"Stay down," the vampire ordered and stalked towards Sameen.

She fought to say something...*anything*...to Regulus, but Freya was too strong, and she could only stare at him, pleading with eyes that struggled to focus and hoping he'd understand she didn't want to do this.

Blood stained his hand, and when she blinked, he disappeared. Or so she thought until he hauled her up from behind, covering her mouth as she tried to scream.

The sweet, coppery tang of blood coated her tongue, and Sameen retched, trying to spit it out, but there was so much. Her stomach roiled, and Freya called forth more fire, but Sameen's body was too weak, and the practitioner cursed her with every foul word she knew.

Sameen prayed the end would be quick. If Regulus drained her, she'd consider her death a good end. One that wouldn't hurt Peter, Cade, Mara...anyone else.

Fangs pierced her neck, and she closed her eyes. Deep in her battered mind, she thought she heard the vampire's voice.

"Take from me. Trust me. Trust your own strength."

Her body obeyed without question, his influence even more powerful than Freya's, and she swallowed the blood filling her mouth and sucked at the fresh wounds on his palm. After a second mouthful, he dropped her, racing away too fast for her to see where he'd gone.

Peter. She had to find Peter. But Freya wouldn't let her. The witch was livid at this little act of rebellion and forced Sameen to take off at a run, right for the stone structure and to the stairs that led to the ritual room.

CHAPTER SEVENTEEN

PETER

His wolf didn't understand what the hell was going on. He'd heard his mate cry out, and when he'd turned, he'd seen Regulus carrying her away from Eli and Caitlin.

The vampire owed him a life debt. One that should have extended to his mate as well. And yet, they'd been battling each other.

Peter tried, once again, to get up, but his shattered left leg wouldn't hold him. He had to shift to heal himself, and that would take time he feared he didn't have. Regulus had *fed* from Sameen. Bitten her and taken her blood, and all Peter could think about was driving a stake through the man's heart.

He reached for his humanity, but before he could shift, Regulus was at his side. "There is no time," the vampire growled, his iron grip holding Peter by the nape of his neck. "The sooth-sayer foretold this. 'Salvation comes from strength of heart. Not of body.' Your mate's body is too weak to fight them. But her heart...that may still triumph. With help. Yours and mine. Drink. I took from her to forge a connection. If you now take from me, you will benefit from that connection as well."

Peter didn't understand and *definitely* didn't want to drink Regulus's blood, but the vampire swore under his breath and held Peter's gaze, using his *glamour* to fucking compel him to lick the blood welling from the open wounds on his palm.

Mara screamed again, and the vampire's head snapped up, his eyes narrowing as he stared at the tower. "Hurry. There is little time."

The blood felt like it was acid flowing through Peter's veins, but his broken leg healed in a few seconds, and he felt stronger than he had in years. He bounded for the castle, marveling at his speed.

No wonder the practitioners targeted vampires for the power of their blood.

He still couldn't understand why Sameen had to fight the Thirteen at all. Eli's casting should have protected her. If she was under their control again—and though he didn't want to believe that were true, why else would she and Regulus have been fighting?—would she survive? Would any of them?

On the second landing, a blast of magic burned the fur on his right shoulder, and his wolf dropped and rolled, coming up across from a door shimmering with a greenish-yellow hue. Paddy held on to the stair rail across from him, his breath sawing in and out of his chest, and inside the large circular room, Liam growled and attacked a woman wearing a light purple robe while Caitlin used her air to drive a second, identically dressed man back ten feet, sending him tumbling out of a window with a scream.

Four more practitioners—or novitiates—*appeared* out of thin air, and a lupine blur—that could only be Ewan—leapt for one of them. Farren, who'd been on her side next to an unconscious, human Tierney, staggered to her feet and growled.

Peter leapt for the doorway, but the magical barrier threw him back, and Paddy stood up a little taller. "Go," the old man wheezed. "Ye're needed at the top. Earth and air must once more pair...and love will offer choice."

What the fuck did that mean? Peter wasn't sure he cared. Not when his mate was up there, along with Cade, Mara, Eli, Regulus, and Livie. Bounding up the steps four at a time, he found all of them together on a landing, with no door to be seen. Eli pressed his hands to the stone.

"They're behind this wall. But it's spelled like nothing I've ever felt before." Staring back at Regulus, he arched his brows. "Well, mate? Want to go at this together?"

"I want nothing of the sort. But we have no choice."

Eli pulled off his shirt and stared down at the markings across his chest. Several of the symbols started to move and twist, and he called on two of his elements.

Earth and Air.

"Earth and air must once more pair."

Fuck. Peter hoped this was what Paddy had been talking about. Regulus drove his shoulder into the stone again and again, shaking the wall with each impact, and together, the two started to chip away at the last barrier between them and their destiny.

***

MARA

Screaming. She was screaming. Her arms ached, and when she tried to rub her eyes, she realized why. She wasn't in the cell anymore.

The ritual space was illuminated with hundreds of candles, and Mara lay on the altar, her arms chained over her head. In the middle of another contraction.

Her cries echoed off the walls, and as she writhed, desperate for a break from the pain, horror washed over her. She was naked, her ankles bound in such a way that her knees were bent and a thick, woven cloth covered her belly and draped over her thighs.

This was all wrong. She should have been with her mate. Her family. Warm and protected and safe. Not lying on hard stone, about to be slain so the Thirteen could use her child in some demented ritual.

"Drink," Celia said, appearing close to her head with a bottle of the green liquid.

Even though she knew she shouldn't, that they were drugging her and the baby, the control they had over her was too strong, and Mara choked down half of it before the practitioner pulled the concoction away and rejoined the semi-circle of witches behind her.

The room shimmered, but the pain started to fade, though whether from the end of the contraction or the drugs, Mara had no idea.

"*We call upon earth, air, fire, and water,*" the practitioners chanted in unison. "*Find your home within this child, and let the power of the spirit consume you.*"

Consume? Consume what? Me? The baby?

Mara tried to pull at the chains, but her body wouldn't listen to her, and another contraction drew a scream from her raw throat.

The entire structure started to shake, like an earthquake deep underground, and across from the practitioners, the stone wall started to crumble.

Was she dreaming? The witches didn't seem to notice. Or care. But then a low, feral growl—followed by another and another—drowned out the chanting, and Mara blinked hard.

Cade. Livie. Peter. They were here. They'd come.

Magic flared, so bright it hurt her eyes, and the urge to push was almost overwhelming. Livie's wolf let out a yelp, and Peter, only a dark streak as he raced across the room, took down one of the men in black and ripped at his throat, only pulling away when his muzzle was dripping with blood.

A ball of yellow light hurtled over Mara's head, hitting Livie, and she collapsed, starting to shift back into human form as Eli burst into the room.

Fire shot from his hand, turning one of the robed men to ash before her eyes.

Do something!

Mara fought against the Thirteen's control, the drugs they'd given her, the total and complete exhaustion of a labor that she could hardly remember, but knew had been going on for hours.

Cade's wolf landed next to her, canines bared.

"Run," she managed. "Trap..."

Her mate snarled, his steely gaze locking with hers. The pure love and devotion in his eyes pulled a sob from her throat. There was no way he'd leave her, and as much as she wanted to escape, to spend the rest of her life with him—and their baby— her hope was fading by the second.

A tall man dressed in a black leather coat crossed the room in a blur and snapped the chains around her wrists and ankles. "Get her out of here," he ordered Cade. "Before she births. Or all will be lost."

He took off again, heading for Celia, and Mara's head lolled to one side as Cade shifted back into his human form.

"Mara? Honey? I'm here," he said and brushed her hair out of her eyes.

Another contraction stole her breath, and she pushed, bearing down with everything she had left. "Ba-by," she managed through gritted teeth.

Cade moved between her bent legs, and his eyes widened. "She's coming...now?"

"No...shit." Tears tumbled down Mara's cheeks, and she only

had time for a single breath before she had to push again. "Cade…"

"It's okay, honey." Cade gripped her knee tightly. "I'm not going anywhere."

You have to run.

Mara tried to tell him. But she couldn't. All she could do was push and pray.

PETER

Livie lay on the floor in human form, blood staining her shoulder and her skin rippling with the start of her shift. Eli slumped against the wall looking dazed, and Regulus held one of the practitioners in front of him like a shield as he bit down on her neck. The woman didn't fight. She was…smiling, and before Peter could bark out a warning, Regulus screamed in pain. He managed to snap her neck before he crumpled to the ground, his skin turning red, then black as he writhed and clawed at his jacket. "Poison…" he whispered.

Too many of them.

Six practitioners and at least four men wearing black robes, their faces covered. Like Eli's father. Slaves. Prisoners. Bound by the control sigils. At least Peter had managed to kill one, and Eli another.

And in the center of the room, Mara lay naked on an altar, her swollen belly so much larger than it had been just days ago. Holy shit. She was in *labor*. Cade stood naked, peering… between her legs. Was the baby coming right now?

The witches were chanting, like they didn't even care there were three werewolves, a practitioner with command of the elements, and a vampire in the room. Or that the rest of Peter's family was battling one floor below, and had looked to be winning—or at least holding their own.

"We call upon earth, air, fire, and water. Find your home within this child, and let the power of the spirit consume you."

Eli crawled to Regulus, sending water and air washing over the vampire, and his screams faded to hoarse grunts as his skin started to heal. Mara cried out, and Cade yelled for her to push.

Peter looked around wildly. His mate. Where was his mate?

Livie growled and landed on one of the robed men, going for his throat as he pulled a knife and tried to slash at her side.

And then Peter saw Sameen. She stood between two of the practitioners, tears streaming down her cheeks, and her eyes filled with horror and pain.

Mara's desperate scream filled the room, followed by a tiny wail, and Cade froze, the baby cradled in his hands.

That's when Sameen stepped forward, her movements jerky, like she was trying with everything she was to fight them, but Peter felt her despair. Her regrets. Her sorrow.

The practitioner in the center, the one who had to be in charge, because her magic outshone all the rest, haloing her in a sickly yellow light, raised her arms. "The conduit will kneel."

Sameen sank down so hard, Peter heard the thunk as her knees hit the ground.

"Celia...she's going to kill me, Peter. I'm sorry..."

He could hear his mate's voice in his head? How?

Regulus. The vampire's connection forged in blood. Could she hear Peter as well?

"I'm coming, sweetheart. Hold on for me."

Peter leapt for his mate, but a blast of magic struck him in the chest, and his fur started to burn. He crumpled, writhing, his worst nightmare come to life. The fire. Being unable to save Ollie. And now Sameen. He let out a hoarse whine, all while Sameen cried and begged Celia to stop.

Eli raced to his side, sending water washing over his fur, but the flames wouldn't stop. How much longer did he have? Long enough to tell Sameen he loved her one last time? A cascading pile of wood and brick landed on him, and while they dampened some of the flames, they broke his ribs, his arm, and his pelvis, and Peter howled.

Cade collapsed, the baby cradled to his chest, but a second practitioner stepped forward, and with a few words in Gaelic, cut the baby's cord, banished the blood and remnants of the birth from Mara, and wrapped the little one up in an ornately patterned piece of fabric as Cade started to shift into his wolf. He growled, then whimpered, and even as Peter burned and struggled to breathe, he understood.

Cade's shift had been brought on by magic, and the alpha couldn't stop it. Couldn't shift back. They'd trapped him again, and it was killing him.

Sunlight flooded the room, despite it being just after midnight, and Regulus hissed and brought his hand up to cover his eyes. Eli's spell kept him from burning, but the momentary distraction was enough for another practitioner to, with a flick of her wrist, conjure silver chains from the air and send them snaking around the vampire's entire body. He fell with a weak curse, and his eyes rolled back in his head.

Next to Peter, Eli sank down on his ass. "Who...who are you? Where are we? I don't remember...who I am."

The flames burned Peter's muzzle. One of his ears felt like it was...gone. And he couldn't move.

"Sameen. I'm so sorry, sweetheart. I love you."

She shook her head, sobbing even harder when Celia grabbed her braid and twisted to expose her neck.

"Bring the mother," Celia said. "Both parents must die when the child absorbs the elements from the conduit and the son of the traitor."

Two more practitioners dragged Mara off the altar and

dropped her next to her mate. She moaned softly, barely managing to stretch out her hand to touch his paw.

All six of the witches started chanting again, and the one next to Celia withdrew a blade from her robes and drove it deep into Mara's back.

Cade howled, the muscles in his neck straining. The magic had not only trapped him as his wolf, but stopped him from moving at all. He could do nothing but watch as Mara shuddered and gasped for breath, blood pooling around her.

"Love...you...shaggy man."

CHAPTER EIGHTEEN

*S*he couldn't move. Celia's magic had trapped her in her own body once more, left her unable to blink, breathe, or even whimper. Tears streamed down her cheeks, and her vision started to blur.

The hazy form of her mate twitched and whined from only ten feet away, most of his body buried under a pile of rubble.

"Not every truth is right..."

Regulus whispered to her mind, but she didn't know what he meant—besides quoting Paddy's words back to her.

"Sameen..."

Peter. Her heart shattered into dust at the agony she felt pouring from him.

"Burning...can't hold on this time. Love you...always."

This time. This time?

A blast of pure, white light sent sparks dancing over the stone floor, and the blood pouring from the wound to Mara's back seemed to disappear wherever one of the pinpricks of magic hit.

"Yer lies do fade when shown the light. Truth now seen will fuel the fight." Paddy. The old man tottered into the room, his eyes glowing, and smiled.

"You think you can stop us?" Celia asked. The other practitioners laughed and Freya pulled an athame from a sheath under her robes and threw it end over end in his direction. It found its mark, burying itself hilt-deep in his stomach, and he stumbled until his back hit the wall, then sank to the floor.

No. Not Paddy. The harmless old man had been kind, despite his ramblings. Blood stained his old tweed jacket, but the wound glowed with the same white light he'd sent towards Mara. It flowed over the stones towards Sameen, curling around her fingers.

More of her tears fell, and as they dripped from her jaw, Sameen understood.

Salvation comes from strength of heart, not of body.

She wasn't locked in her own body. Not truly. Not completely. If she were...she wouldn't be able to cry. Peter was burning, crushed under rubble. Cade was trapped as his wolf, watching his mate die. Eli didn't know who he was, and Regulus struggled to free himself from silver chains—one of the only ways to weaken or kill a vampire.

What if none of these tortures were actually real? If Sameen could move, maybe the others could escape their nightmares as well.

Celia placed the baby in the center of the altar. "You will be ours, little one. Now and forever." Tracing the control sigil over the infant, she sealed the casting by drawing a sharp fingernail along her palm and letting a drop of her blood land on the newborn's forehead.

No. You can't have her. She's Mara's!

Cade obviously agreed with Sameen, because the wolf growled with such anger, it seemed to fill the room.

The group of practitioners started to chant in Gaelic, and Eli fell over, his arms and legs twitching as he screamed. His back arched, and the tower rumbled underneath them. Sameen couldn't let them take his earth. He wouldn't survive. No earth elemental ever lived after losing their element.

A thin stream of dust escaped his lips, swirled around the room, and settled over the baby until the little girl let out a wail. When she stopped to inhale, she absorbed the element, and her tiny body shuddered.

Sameen screamed, even though no sound escaped her paralyzed lips. She could do this. *Salvation comes from strength of heart. Strength of heart.*

Her love for Peter. She focused on him, on his eyes, on his pained whimpers and yips as he struggled to free himself from the pile of burning rubble.

"I love you. Fight for me. It's all in our heads. Our worst nightmares. You can escape this. So can I."

The practitioners turned towards Sameen, and the collective power of their magic hit her square in the chest. All the elemental fragments inside her fought to escape, and the pain… it was like nothing she'd ever experienced. Worse by far than any time the Thirteen had tortured her. Worse than not being able to blink for months or even years. Worse than knowing she was nothing but an object. Worse than losing her freedom a second time.

Air fought its way free first, unseen until it wrapped itself around the baby, lifted her a few inches off the altar, and gently set her back down. Water followed in the form of Sameen's tears, landing on those pale, chubby cheeks and making the child scream even louder.

Fire crackled over Sameen's skin, blistering and burning her fingers yet again, and heading straight for the altar. As the last vestige of elemental power left her, Sameen crumpled to the stone floor, her heartbeat slowing, unable to breathe, and knowing that in seconds, she'd die.

Flames spun in a circle over the baby. Mara begged for her child's life, her voice so weak Sameen could hardly hear her, and Cade howled.

"Not every truth is right..." Paddy rasped, his pale lips coated with blood.

Sameen pulled in half a breath, fearing it might be her last, and stared at her mate. *"Protect the baby..."*

* * *

PETER

The fire element that bitch had pulled out of his mate was heading right for the Mara's child. Peter growled, kicking his back legs hard enough to loosen the heaviest beam. It tumbled off the pile and...disappeared?

It's all in our heads.

Sameen's words. He'd heard her, but he hadn't understood. Yes, this was his worst nightmare, but that made it no less real. The pain of his pelt burning, of his broken ribs, his cracked pelvis, the stench of smoke and blood all around him...

Everything the old man had said. Every word over months and months suddenly made sense. Peter scrambled to his feet, the rubble vanishing before his eyes, and jumped with every last bit of energy he could muster. The swirling fire element shot into Mara and Cade's baby just as Peter closed his jaws around the material swaddling her.

He landed next to Cade, placed the baby against Mara's side, and grabbed his alpha by the neck. *"Move!"* he growled at Cade, and shock—if nothing else—got Cade's legs under him. Regulus broke free from the practitioners' illusion and flew towards the closest witch, snapping her neck before Peter could even blink.

"Rachel…" Mara's faint whisper stopped Cade in his tracks. "The blood…"

The alpha wolf gently pawed at his daughter's forehead, wiping away the drop of Celia's blood marring her pink skin. With a howling cry, the little girl flailed against the swaddling, her cheeks turning bright crimson. The fine wisps of blond hair covering her head caught fire, and the walls around them started to crumble. Raindrops pelted the group, washing away the blood pooling around Mara, and lending a glow to the water elemental's skin.

A gust of wind caught Celia off guard, and the witch flew back ten feet. Regulus killed a second practitioner and Cade tackled a third. Peter reached Sameen's side and pressed his nose to her neck.

Come on, sweetheart. Wake up. Fight.

All four elements battled one another, fiery explosions landing within inches of the practitioners, rocks falling from the ceiling, and blasts of air knocking the last two men wearing black robes onto their asses.

Sameen's eyes fluttered, and Peter whined. *"Please. Look at me."*

"Regulus," she managed. "Need him…and Paddy. Help me."

He was useless as his wolf. Regulus couldn't understand him, and Paddy…the man was dying. Sameen struggled to push up on an elbow, and Peter lay on his belly, reaching for his humanity. The shift shattered his bones, and with the memory of the fire and being trapped under the rubble so fresh in his mind, he almost gave up. But Sameen needed him.

His muscles shook with the aftereffects of the shift. "Regulus! Get your ass over here."

The vampire was at their side before Peter even finished the sentence. "What is it?"

"The blood of the stone," Sameen said as Peter helped her to her feet. "The practitioner told Cade what he needed to save Mara. Find the blood of the stone. It's Paddy. In a way."

Regulus wrapped an arm around each of them and they moved so quickly, Peter's stomach lurched and Sameen buried her face against his neck.

"Never...again," she moaned when the vampire set them down and knelt next to the dying man.

"I second that." The idea of another man's hands on his mate had his wolf clawing to be let loose, but this wasn't the time. Not when Eli was in the center of an elemental storm like nothing he'd ever seen, and Livie was dodging stones and balls of flame trying to get to him.

Liam, Farren, Tierney, and Ewan bounded into the room, all in wolf form, with Caitlin just behind them. "Oh, my God." The air elemental raced to Mara, who was curled over her daughter, blood still trickling from the wound in her back, with Cade's wolf scanning for any incoming threat. A ball of fire hit his flank, and he yelped, but didn't back down. Caitlin called on her air to dampen the flames, then conjured a spinning shield from her element to protect the four of them.

The wolves went after the practitioners one by one with Eli in the center of the room, the symbols inked on his skin in constant motion. His eyes were closed, his mouth open in a silent scream, and Farren's wolf howled as she reared up on her back legs and pawed at his cheek. He didn't respond. Didn't even flinch.

"Eli is going to die if we can't get the elements to combine." Sameen cupped Paddy's cheek. "But Paddy...he won't. Not if Regulus can seal the wound and get him into the center of that vortex."

"What? Sameen, there's no way Paddy's going to make it."

"I concur," Regulus said. "He has lost too much blood. The only way he will go on is if I turn him, and," the vampire leaned close to the old man and sniffed, "he is not human. I do not think turning him is an option."

"Trust me, please. Seal the wound and get him close to Eli. He'll do the rest." Sameen turned to Peter and held his gaze. "I know who I am now, Peter. I *am* the conduit. Or…I was. I failed the Thirteen every time because they could never get Earth to be stable inside me. But the baby…she held all four elements. And now…they're free with nowhere to go. Paddy doesn't have the blood of the stone. He *is* the bloodstone. It's the stone of balance. He can channel the elements in to Eli. Safely."

Caitlin shouted, "'The one ya' seek hides in plain sight.' He wasn't afraid to die tonight. Because he knew he wouldn't. Get him over there!"

Regulus bared his fangs and pierced his index finger as Peter slid the athame from Paddy's gut. The vampire dragged his bloody finger along the wound, and it sealed in seconds. "If this is my end, ancient one, I will be very pissed off."

Paddy blinked up at the vampire and smiled, his lips bloody and his skin deathly pale. "Trust your elder, vampire."

Elder?

Peter gaped as Regulus hauled Paddy to his feet and took off, the two of them nothing but a blur.

"How…?" Peter asked. He kept Sameen tucked against him and tried to stay low as they dashed for Cade, Mara, Caitlin, and the baby.

"She burst into flames," Mara sobbed, rocking her daughter gently as the infant wailed in her arms. The fine hair matted to her head glowed and occasionally set off an errant spark, and Sameen reached out and let the baby take hold of her finger.

Almost immediately, the little girl stopped fussing, and her skin went from bright red to a healthy, newborn pink. Sameen's eyelids fluttered, flames glowing in the depths of her irises for a brief moment until she blinked and Peter found only the pale brown orbs he'd come to love.

"What...?" Mara asked, choking back a sob and staring down at her daughter's peaceful face.

Before Sameen could answer, Eli screamed, and they all turned to the center of the room. The symbols for the elements on his chest glowed pure white, and Paddy stood facing him, a great ball of energy growing ever larger between them.

Regulus held Farren's wolf back, and she snapped and strained against him, trying to get to her mate, while Livie, Ewan, Tierney, and Liam stood over the bodies of the last of the practitioners. All of them dead save one.

"Celia," Sameen whispered. "No!"

CHAPTER NINETEEN

SAMEEN

*H*ow could Celia still be alive?

Paddy and Eli were locked together now, each man's hands clasped around the other's forearms. Farren howled and whined, desperate to get to her mate, and the rest of the wolves watched with a mixture of awe and horror at the scene in front of them.

Sameen and Peter were the only ones who seemed to notice Celia was moving. Not quickly. Not without immense pain if her expression were anything to go by. But the witch was most definitely alive.

"If she escapes," Sameen whispered to Peter, "I'll never be free."

"She won't." He lowered himself to all fours. "Stay here with Mara, Cade, and the baby. If she doesn't see you, maybe she'll forget about you."

Hardly.

Celia knew exactly where she was. Sameen could feel it. As

Peter's bones cracked and his skin darkened in to a thick pelt, the sigil on her side started to burn. "Caitlin. Please," Sameen whispered. "I need your help."

Peter slunk off, keeping to the edges of the room as Caitlin clutched Sameen's hand. "Anythin', luv. Ya' risked everythin' for us."

Pulling up her tank top, Sameen struggled against Celia's call. The witch wanted her to take the baby. To snatch it away from Mara and bring it to the center of the ritual space where Eli and Paddy were currently locked together.

And if she couldn't get Sameen to do it, Mara would be the next one she called to. "Cut it. Scar it. Do *something*. Anything. For me...and Mara."

Cade growled and got between Mara and the other two women. Despite not speaking wolf, Sameen knew exactly what those vocalizations meant. *No one touches my mate. I'll kill them first.*

"She's right," Mara said. The water elemental slumped against the wall, her child calm for the first time since Celia had set her on the altar. But Mara looked like she was about to pass out. "She...wants the baby. I don't...I'm not strong enough to fight her. Not after...she drugged me. Rachel too."

This time, Cade's snarl took on a deadly warning. Torn between protecting his family and ripping Celia's head off, he nudged Caitlin's shoulder and yipped.

The air elemental reached for the athame Peter had pulled out of Paddy and brushed it off on her pants. "This is going to hurt," Caitlin said.

"I just had a baby. Without an epidural," Mara muttered. "After being branded, drugged, and chained to an altar. I can handle this."

Sameen grit her teeth and closed her eyes. At least Caitlin was quick. Two cuts. Deep ones. They stung, then started to burn, and when her blood flowed, seeping into the waistband of her pants, she jammed her fist against her mouth to stifle her scream.

Across from her, Mara handled the pain much better, though Cade pressed his entire body against his mate and let her snake an arm around his neck. The wolf nuzzled the baby's head as Caitlin cut across the half circle that represented the Thirteen's magic.

As soon as the connection had been severed, Sameen felt like a giant weight had been lifted from her shoulders. She had a chance now. A real chance. If they escaped this room...she could be free.

Celia rose to her knees, a green ball of magic growing ever larger between her hands.

No. Sameen knew that spell. It would kill Peter in an instant. Scrambling to her feet, she ignored the pain and pushed herself as hard as she could, leaping at the last minute and tackling Peter's wolf.

The spell hit her in the shoulder, and her entire right side went numb, but she'd protected the man she loved, and that was all she cared about.

Cade growled, long and low and feral, and bounded for Celia. His massive paws hit Celia's neck, and the snap of her spinal column reached Sameen's ears just as Peter nuzzled her cheek and whined.

"I'm sorry, Peter. Your family...needed you. I'm free now."

The wolf pawed at the ground, then leaned in and bit Sameen's shoulder. The sound he made...it was almost *please*.

"I want to live, Peter. I want a life. With you. But...it's all right. Because I'll die free." She stopped fighting, truly relaxing for the first time since before she'd been taken. Peter's howl was the last sound she heard, and she smiled. "Love...you."

PETER

Hell, no. He was not going to lose his mate now. Calling for Regulus, hoping the vampire could understand him, he lay down next to Sameen and rested his muzzle over her heart. When Regulus took a knee next to him, he frowned. "I am beginning to think the only reason you want me around is to resurrect your dying."

Peter growled, and Regulus patted his shoulder with his mangled hand.

"Watch, wolf. And never forget the miracle that is your mate."

That's when Peter realized the conflagration that had only moments ago been ready to consume the entire space, had faded into nothing.

Eli lay on his side with Farren, naked as the day she was born wrapped around him, tears in her eyes and a harsh expression on her face. "If you ever do that again, *mo grá,* I will find a way to lock you in our bedroom for at least a month."

"I'd like to see you try." His voice didn't hold its usual strength, but he was very much alive. So was Paddy. The old man slung an arm around Tierney's sleek lupine body and let the wolf steady him. Only Ewan, now back in human form, looked at all unsettled.

"Sire…the hunger…"

Regulus rushed over to the boy and held his gaze. "I forbid you from feeding until we return to the plane. The witches are poison to us, and the rest…they are family. We will go together, and after you have fed, we will bring back clothing and medical supplies."

"Do not leave. Any of you," Regulus ordered. "No magic bearer remains alive in this structure, but there may be some of the Thirteen's supporters close by. Ewan and I will return in less than five minutes. Stick together, and should trouble arise, Eli? I trust you understand this new power inside you enough to defend everyone?"

Eli, with Farren's help, sat up and held out his hand. A luminous, glowing teardrop hovered above his palm, and he sent it drifting towards Sameen. It found her shoulder, spreading out to form a gauzy film over her right side. And before Peter's eyes, it soaked into her jacket, into the soft skin of her neck, into the tight black pants that clung to her slim frame.

For ten seconds—he counted each one—nothing happened, and then her heart started to beat. He made an inquisitive sound, and when he raised his head, her eyes were open. A deep, dark brown greeted him, and she blinked hard. "Peter. I...see you. All of you. Oh, God. And the fire...what I siphoned off from Mara's baby...it's at peace."

Peter shifted back into a man, even though he hated taking even a single, distracted second away from his mate. But he needed to hold her. Talk to her. Tell her he loved her.

"Sameen? Is this really true? All of it?"

She didn't answer in words, but by throwing her arms around him and kissing him. No hesitation. No fear. And though every one of their past kisses had been nothing but perfection in his mind, this one...this one was so much more.

CHAPTER TWENTY

PETER

*R*egulus and Ewan were as good as their word,
returning in under five minutes with a large duffel
bag full of clothing, bottles of water, and a fully stocked first
aid kit.

Sameen hadn't stopped staring at him since she'd opened her
eyes. A few locks of hair had escaped her braid, and Peter
reached over to tuck one behind her ear.

"How did you know?" he asked. "About Paddy?"

She settled closer to him, resting her head on his shoulder as
Livie—the only one of them to have a clue what to do after
giving birth—tended to Mara. The water elemental had been
drugged before they'd found her, and was mostly out of it, with
Cade cradling their newborn, a mixture of awe and terror in his
eyes.

"I listened," Sameen said quietly. "All those years trapped by
their magic...they never let me sleep. I was awake the whole
time. Not always aware, but awake."

"Fuck, sweetheart. So the night I found you..."

"That was the first time I'd slept in twelve years." Wiping away a tear, she shook her head, as if banishing yet another demon from her memories. "They talked in front of me. Never bothered to hide their plans. Why would they? I couldn't escape, couldn't speak. I never paid much attention. My mind was too broken. All I wanted was to die. But some of their ramblings stayed with me."

"Still...Paddy being the blood of the stone? Or bloodstone? I don't even know what the hell that means."

"Bloodstones bring unity. I could never form Spirit for the Thirteen. Every time they tried to use my body as the vessel, they failed. Earth...that was the one element they could never force into me."

"And they thought they could force it into Mara's baby?" Peter didn't understand anything that had happened since they'd left Regulus's mansion beyond the fact that his mate was in his arms, whole, and every member of their family had miraculously survived.

"Rachel isn't just an elemental," Sameen replied. "She's fire born of water and a werewolf too. That makes her stronger than any of us."

"Then why didn't she become Spirit? Why did it have to be Eli?"

Glancing over at Cade, Mara, and the baby, Sameen smiled. "Because Rachel wanted her mother. The two of them...they're linked. They always will be."

"But Paddy...?"

The old man chuckled. "What was never meant to exist will be the salvation of all."

Peter narrowed his eyes at Paddy and scowled. "Is that supposed to clear things up for me?"

Getting to his feet with a groan, Paddy shuffled to the center of the room. "What was hidden will be revealed." He closed his eyes, and burst into flames. The fire consumed him in the space of a breath, but no heat spread through the room, no smoke, no scent of burning flesh.

As quickly as it had started, the swirling conflagration disappeared, leaving a slightly younger version of Paddy behind. His clothes hadn't changed—the tweed jacket not even singed, and his hair was still pure white, but when he smiled, he had a mouthful of crooked teeth and his eyes held every color of the rainbow.

"Fuck me. Hurts every time," he said.

"Wait. That wasn't a riddle." Farren leapt to her feet and stalked over to the old man. "Ya' mean to tell me ya' could talk like a normal human bein' this whole feckin' time? What in the bloody hell are ya'? And don't start spoutin' more nonsense."

Regulus passed Paddy a bottle of water. "He is the lone offspring of the Fae Queen Titania and the first Phoenix shifter."

"Holy shit. So seeing your end again and again..." Peter said.

"I have died more times than any other livin' creature." With a sigh, Paddy headed for the wall Regulus and Eli had destroyed to enter the ritual space. "And yet, I cannot rest." He turned back to the group. "Farren? I do not know if our paths will cross again. But if ya' need me, I will hear yer call."

The female alpha ran to the old man and threw her arms around him. "Don't say that, ya' daft bastard. Stay."

He embraced her, his multi-hued eyes shimmering with tears. "The Fates send me where I need to be. Each time, I'm a different man. But always with the same memories. I'll never forget ya', my silver wolf." With a fatherly kiss to the top of her head, Paddy released her. "I'll leave ya' with one more riddle, lass. *Purpose found is worth the wait. More so when ya' keep the faith. Rules are fine when sense they make, but ne're forget what's at stake. Love and trust are precious, true, for strength of heart finds those too few.*"

Before Farren could curse at him or ask him to explain, he darted from the room. She rushed after him, but two steps onto the landing, stopped with a choked sob. "He's gone."

Eli draped his arm around her shoulders. "I don't think that man is ever truly gone. When you need him, he'll be there."

The baby cooed in Mara's arms, and Cade cleared his throat. "Can we all get the fuck out of here now?"

Livie elbowed him in the side. "Language, bossman. That little one is going to start talking before you know it."

The alpha wolf gazed at his mate and baby daughter, love shining in his eyes. "I don't care what her first word is. Having her and Mara back alive and safe? Knowing my family—my *entire* family—is intact? That's all that really matters."

Peter helped Sameen to her feet. "He's including you too, you know," he said quietly as Cade scooped Mara and Rachel into his arms. "You're part of this family. If you want to be."

Her brown eyes shone as she brushed her fingers over his scarred cheek. "There's a lot I still don't know about who I am, Peter."

His heart threatened to beat right out of his chest. Was she rejecting him? He wouldn't force her. Though begging wasn't out of the question.

"But I know I love you. The rest...we can figure it out as we go. Right?" She smiled up at him, and for the first time since the fire, he didn't feel so broken. She'd healed him in ways he'd not known were possible, and he'd spend the rest of his life loving her back.

"Together, sweetheart, I think we can do anything." He dipped his head, and when they kissed, the rest of the world fell away, and he and his wolf found what they'd been searching for since the day he'd been bitten.

Peace.

EPILOGUE

PETER

Two steps inside the back door, and the scent of chocolate hit him square in the face. Followed by the sound of his mate's laughter.

"What are you doing? They're not ready yet!"

"This oven may be top of the line, but it's as daft as my great aunt. Stick the toothpick in the center of the pan. If it comes out clean, they're done," Tierney said.

"Seriously? The directions on the box said thirty minutes. It's only been twenty-eight." His mate's confusion was adorable. Over the past week, the pack—both packs—had started to heal.

Mara, Cade, and the baby spent most of their time in their room, and Peter worried for the three of them, but the few times Cade had emerged to grab a tray of food, he'd assured them that Mara just needed a few more days to recover.

Tierney had taken it upon himself to teach Sameen how to bake and use the computer. He never touched her—Peter threatened him with bodily harm the first time he'd found the two of them in the open kitchen with Sameen eating more chocolate chips than were going into the bowl of cookie dough —but Sameen had taken to the young wolf like a brother.

Especially after Tierney had revealed an eye for fashion he'd never admitted to anyone. When the first parcel of clothing had arrived for Sameen, she'd spent an hour locked in their bedroom before she'd let Peter in. He'd found her wearing a pair of loose, flowing pants in a rich blue, a cream blouse tied at her right shoulder, and a long golden sweater.

The confidence of finding her own style had done wonders for her, and she no longer kept silent during meals or hid behind Peter when the other wolves came into the room.

"What are you two doing?" Peter asked as he peered around the corner.

"Brownies!" Sameen held up the toothpick. "They're done. Apparently."

"Well, they have to cool before ya' can eat them." Tierney dodged the dish cloth Sameen threw at him. "It's either that or ye'll burn yer tongue and won't taste anythin'—includin' the brownies—for two days."

Peter finished buttoning his shirt—Liam and Shawn had asked him to run with them—and slid an arm around his mate's waist. "I can think of a few ways we could pass the time."

Making vague choking sounds, Tierney shooed them out of the kitchen. "If ye're goin' to get naked, do it in yer own room. I've supper to put on once Christine gets back from the store."

The day after they'd put an end to the Thirteen, the rest of the pack—Shawn and Serena, Christine, and Ollie—had flown into Glasgow, and though Regulus grumbled at the sheer number of people in his house, the vampire honestly seemed to enjoy the company. When he wasn't helping Ewan learn to control his urges.

"Come on, sweetheart. Let's give the man some space to work."

Despite Tierney's assumption, Peter and Sameen hadn't done more than kiss yet. Well, there'd been some groping. Perhaps a bit of grinding. But she hadn't been ready for more.

It didn't matter how much his balls ached or how many times he'd rubbed one out in the shower after her nerves had gotten the best of her. Peter would wait for her forever if that's what she needed.

"Can we talk? About...the future?" he asked when they reached their room and Sameen immediately went to the window and parted the drapes. She *needed* to see the sky whenever she could, and when the power had gone out after a bad storm two nights ago and they'd woken to complete darkness, the terror in her voice...it had shattered him.

"About the mating? I already told you—"

"No. Not about that." Peter joined her at the window, linking their fingers as they both stared out over the manicured lawn to the tree line. "Farren lost most of her pack when we were fighting Fergus. Two, he killed, and the third...well, we might never know. All she has left are Tierney and Ewan, and neither of them want to be her beta. Ewan...well, even if he did want it, him being a vampire and all...it complicates things."

"I don't understand." Sameen turned to face him, her dark brows furrowed. "What does that have to do with us?"

"Farren asked me to be her beta." As he said the words, he straightened, the sense of pride he'd felt all day both baffling and rewarding. "I shouldn't accept. I wasn't born a wolf. That's the rule. But she seems to think the rules don't matter."

"I thought wolves didn't usually change packs once they'd picked one. That's what Tierney said."

"We don't. But..." Peter stared down at the floor, at the hem of his jeans brushing his bare feet. "I wasn't the easiest guy to live with after the fire. Not after we got Cade back, not when Caitlin showed up after Katerina had forced her to kidnap Mara..." He ran a hand through his hair and lifted his gaze to meet his mate's. "We're a family. They forgave me long ago. But forgiving and forgetting are two different things, and while I'd give my life for any being in this house...I talked to Liam and Shawn today. They gave me their blessing. And Cade gave his before Farren made the offer."

"Would that mean we...have to move?" Fear darkened her eyes, and she gripped his fingers tighter. "I was just getting used to—"

"No." Peter slid his hand up to cup the back of her head and ghosted his lips over hers. "Farren...she wants to stay here. There are too many memories for her back in Doolin. But even though we've two packs in this house, we're all one family. Cade's pack—" He stopped, the very idea he wasn't part of Cade's pack anymore so foreign to him, it brought a lump to his throat. "Cade's pack would move back to Dublin. Into Liam's family estate. Seattle has too many bad memories for Mara now, and Doolin has too many for Caitlin and Liam. Dublin...it's a fresh start for everyone, and it's only an hour's flight."

"So, Farren and Eli, Tierney, Ewan, and the two of us?" she asked.

"And Regulus. He's not pack, and he wouldn't be here all the time. I've never met a man who loves his travel more. But he'd stay for a while. Until Ewan's stable, and he promised to come back often."

Sameen fell quiet, and nerves tightened in Peter's gut. "If you want to go somewhere else, just the two of us, or if you'd feel more comfortable if I stayed with Cade's pack, I'll do it, Sameen. There's nothing I wouldn't do for you."

"I don't know enough of the world to tell you there's nowhere else I'd rather go," she said quietly. "But I do know I feel at home here. Farren's warmed up to me, Tierney's like my big brother—even though I think I'm older than he is—and while Regulus still scares the crap out of me, I trust him after he helped me when Celia...when she..."

"Shhh. Don't go there, sweetheart. She's dead, and we survived."

Sameen nodded and snuggled against his chest, her ear pressed to his heart. "You're my home, Peter. Wherever you are is where I want to be."

***

LATE THAT NIGHT, after dinner and two helpings of Sameen's brownies, Peter led her up the stairs, his entire plan to snuggle with her in the massive bed and introduce her to her very first superhero movie.

But as he opened the wooden panels that hid the flatscreen from view, his mate emerged from the bathroom, and the remote fell from his hand to bounce along the thick carpeting.

A silk sheath in a bright teal draped her body, dipping low between her breasts and falling to mid-thigh. The hard points of her nipples under the silk drew his gaze, and when he was finally able to look up, he found her lips parted, and desire churning in her eyes.

"Sameen...?"

"I know it's not the full moon." She took a single step closer, and he wanted to sweep her into his arms, but this had to be her decision. She'd been through too much, and as she couldn't remember if she'd ever had sex before, the woman who stood in front of him was essentially a virgin. "But, I'm ready."

"Are you sure?"

"Maybe." Her nervous laugh didn't reassure him, but then she reached for his hand and led him to the bed. "I don't know what to do."

"You don't have to do a thing, sweetheart. Just tell me if anything I do makes you uncomfortable."

Peter shucked his jeans and flannel shirt, leaving him in a pair of black briefs, stretched out with his back against the headboard, then patted the mattress. He and Sameen slept together every night, her in one of his t-shirts, him in his briefs. But this was different. This...there was no going back from this.

Sameen fitted herself to his side and he cupped her cheek, tipping her head so he could press a chaste kiss to her lips. She draped her arm around his shoulders and kissed him back, and by the time she pulled away, he could scent her arousal, and his cock strained against the cotton barrier between them.

She'd seen him naked. Felt him. Even palmed his length in the shower the previous morning, a move that almost had him slipping and cracking his head open—and would have been completely worth the injury had he not been able to steady himself.

Peter trailed his hand down her side, careful to avoid the scar she'd bear for the rest of her life. The sigil held no power now. Destroyed when Caitlin had sliced through it in two places, it would never be more than a painful reminder of what his mate had endured.

At her hip, he froze. She wasn't wearing panties. "Sameen?"

"Touch me." She'd pressed her legs together as they'd kissed, as if she was desperate for the friction, the pressure right at her sweet spot, and now she shifted to allow his fingers to slip underneath the gown and find her slick heat. "Oh, God. That's..."

"Too much?" He froze, two fingers between her lower lips, until she let out a shuddering breath.

"More."

Oh, he'd give her more. He'd give her everything. "One day soon, I'm going to have you on your back and bury my face between your thighs until you're screaming my name. But for tonight, we're taking it slow."

Slow turned out to be the wrong word. As soon as he scored his teeth over the spot on her neck that would—on the full moon—forever mark her as his, she came against his hand, trying desperately to keep her little moans and whimpers from turning into full-fledged screams.

Peter held her through her release, through the tremors and the shivers that wracked her body as she came down from the high of her first climax.

"That...wasn't what I expected." Her lids started to droop—she tired so easily still as she worked to strengthen muscles unused for more than a decade—and she let out a heavy sigh. "We're not done, are we?"

"You're exhausted. There's more. So much more I want to experience with you. But we have the rest of our lives together, Sameen. Sleep with me, and maybe in the morning, we'll try for round two."

She didn't respond, and as he listened to her heartbeat, her breathing, he chuckled softly. His mate had already nodded off, and Peter brought his fingers to his lips, tasting her. "I promise to always protect you. Always love you. Always let you be...exactly who you want to be. Until my last breath."

Sealing his vow with a gentle kiss, he pulled the blankets up over them, and when he dreamed, it was of her. It was always of her.

MARA

The nightmare woke her like they always did. With the scars on her side burning and Celia's voice in her head. Demanding Mara bring her the baby. Driving the knife into Mara's back. Forcing her mate to shift into his wolf and then trapping him there—just like her sister had once done.

At least she'd managed not to scream this time. Rolling over, her body still sore, even after a week of rest, she stifled her wince as she focused on her daughter. Rachel slept peacefully in the bassinet next to the bed, and Cade...he stood watch over her.

"You're awake," Mara said. "Is something wrong?"

"I missed so much." Cade shook his head and ran a hand through his unkempt hair. "Five weeks we should have had together. Five weeks I should have been able to talk to her every day, tell her how much I wanted to meet her, how I hoped she'd have your hair, your smile, your eyes." He swallowed hard, and a tear raced down his cheek. "And five days I should have protected *you*."

"Cade. Don't." If he lost it, so would she, and most days, she was barely keeping it together. Between the exhaustion of a newborn, learning how to breastfeed, and wondering if—or when—her baby would burst into flames again, she wasn't sure she had the strength to keep going if her mate broke down.

"Honey..." Cade skirted the bassinet and climbed into bed next to her. "When they took you, I couldn't..."

Mara cupped his cheek. "Look at me, shaggy man. Right now." He turned his steely blue gaze on her, and the punch of power reassured her like nothing else could. She hadn't felt much of anything since she'd been taken besides fear and despair. "You found me. Found us. And Rachel...she's perfect."

"Regulus has a full gym down in the basement of the east wing. Punching bags strong enough for a vampire to take out their aggressions." Cade hunched his shoulders. "I destroyed two of them."

"Two?" Mara stifled her laugh, then her wince as the wounds to her side protested the sudden movement.

"Didn't talk to anyone for two days. Hid down there punching those fucking bags until I was so tired I couldn't stay awake, passed out, then woke up to start all over again. Until Livie showed up and told me to get my head out of my ass."

This time, Mara laughed so hard, the pain sent her collapsing back against the pillows. "Remind me...to thank her."

"Just breathe, honey." Cade pulled up her tank top and peered at the healing wounds. "Let me get Christine."

"No." How could she explain to her mate, to the man she loved more than her own life, that this pain was hers to bear? That it was penance for her sister's death, for failing to protect their baby, for not realizing what was happening to her sooner when her sister's fire—and part of her sister's soul—started taking control of her. "I'm okay, shaggy man. Or...I will be. It's just going to take some time."

Cade wrapped his arms around her, and she couldn't keep her tears from falling any longer. Her mate's hoarse sobs mirrored her own, and they cried until Rachel let out a tiny wail, demanding food and changing, before falling asleep in her daddy's arms.

THE NEXT NIGHT was the first time Cade, Mara, and Rachel joined the rest of the pack for dinner. The baby slept nestled in a sling on Mara's chest, and though she was exhausted and didn't contribute much to the conversation, she found herself smiling more and more as the meal went on, enjoying the comfort of family.

When Tierney tried to get Serena, Livie and Shawn's daughter, to take a bite of mashed potatoes, the little girl spit them out with a look of horror on her round face, then lunged for a bite of steak on Shawn's plate instead.

This time, Mara's laugh didn't hurt as much, and the relief it brought to Cade's face? Worth the discomfort.

"This one hates anything that even resembles a vegetable now," Livie said and turned to Shawn. "I was gone for all of a week and you turned our pup into a carnivore."

"She's just going through a growth spurt." Shawn handed the baby to his mate and tried offering her a pea. Serena batted it away, then reached her arms out for Mara and screamed.

"No, honey. Aunt Mara's got her hands full."

More screaming ensued until Mara artfully extracted Rachel from the sling and passed her to Cade. "I haven't held my niece in months. Come here, you little stinkbug."

As soon as Serena's head tucked under Mara's chin and the little girl calmed and started sucking her thumb, Mara burst into tears.

"Honey, what's wrong?" The terror in Cade's voice infused the entire room, and everyone held their breath.

"Nothing," she sobbed. "Nothing at all."

Serena snuggled closer, and Mara swept her gaze around the large dining room table. Even Regulus had joined them, sipping from a stoneware wine glass Mara was pretty sure wasn't any vintage she wanted to taste.

"I didn't think I'd ever have this again," she said when she finally calmed enough to take a steady breath. "Dinner with family. It's the simplest thing ever, but...to me...this is everything."

Cade rocked Rachel gently in his arms and leaned in to press a kiss to Mara's temple. "I love you, honey. And you're right. Family *is* everything."

***

THANK you for reading the Elemental Shifter series. This was a labor of true love for me. Cade and Mara? They're still one of the most perfect and intriguing couples I've ever had the pleasure of knowing.

With each book, my love of these characters grew. So much so that I don't want to ever let them go. Regulus will get a book one of these days. Ewan and Tierney too. And of course, since packs are family, you'll get updates on all the other werewolves and elementals you've come to love.

You can find an extended *series* epilogue on my website. Just go to https://patriciadeddy.com/BonusContent and enter the password SECRETSTUFF. You'll find bonus content for several of my books there, so if you want to avoid spoilers, don't click on the links for books you haven't read yet!

ABOUT THE AUTHOR

I've always made up stories. Sometimes I even acted them out. I probably shouldn't admit that my childhood best friend and I used to run around the backyard pretending to fly in our Invisible Jet and rescue Steve Trevor. Oops.

Now that I'm too old to spin around in circles with felt magic bracelets on my wrists, I put "pen to paper" instead. Figuratively, at least. Fingers to keyboard is more accurate.

Outside of my writing, I'm a professional editor, a software geek, a singer (in the shower only), and a runner. I love red wine, scotch (neat, please), and cider. Seattle is my home, and I share an old house with my husband and cats.

I'm on my fourth—fifth?—rewatching of the modern *Doctor Who*, and I think one particular quote from that show sums up my entire life.

"We're all stories, in the end. Make it a good one, eh?" — *The Eleventh Doctor, Doctor Who*

I hope your story is brilliant.

You can reach me all over the web...
patriciadeddy.com
patricia@patriciadeddy.com

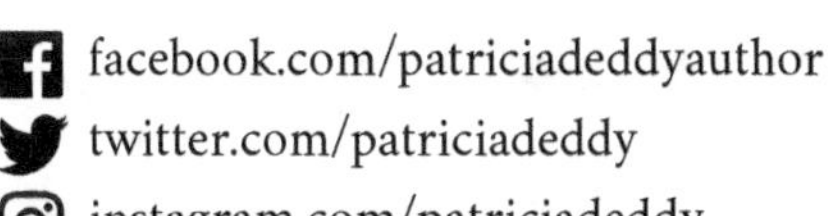

facebook.com/patriciadeddyauthor
twitter.com/patriciadeddy
instagram.com/patriciadeddy

DARK PNR

These novellas will take you into the darker side of the paranormal with vampires, witches, angels, demons, and more.

Forever Kept

Immortal Hunter

Wicked Omens

Storm of Sin

BY THE FATES

Check out the COMPLETE By the Fates series if you love dark and steamy tales of witches, devils, and an epic battle between good and evil.

By the Fates, Freed

Destined: A By the Fates Story

By the Fates, Fought

By the Fates, Fulfilled

IN BLOOD

If you love hot Italian vampires and and a human who can hold her own against beings far stronger, then the In Blood series is for you.

Secrets in Blood

Revelations in Blood

HOLIDAYS AND HEROES

Beauty isn't only skin deep and not all scars heal. Come swoon over sexy vets and the men and women who love them.

Mistletoe and Mochas

Love and Libations

RESTRAINED

Do you like to be tied up? Or read about characters who do? Enjoy a fresh COMPLETE BDSM series that will leave you begging for more.

In His Silks

Christmas Silks

All Tied Up For New Year's

In His Collar